DAVE'S TUNE

June Rayfield Welch

G.L.A. Press
Dallas

Library of Congress Catalog Card
Number 73-84217

ISBN 0-912854-04-4

Printed
by

Waco, Texas

For my father, Frank Albert Welch, and my mother, Elzina Prigmore Welch, who remember such a time and a similar place.

LAWTON, TEXAS

Lawton, in the summer of 1944, was just another Texas town helping to win the war. The young men — with a few exceptions, such as R. L. West, who had a good excuse, and Levi Hackley, who did not — had gone off to fight; women and high school boys had taken over most of the jobs they had vacated.

North of town, on Red River, was Camp John B. Norris, named for some Spanish-American War general. Two infantry divisions were in training there. Service command troops operated the camp and guarded the Italian and German prisoners of war; most had United States Army fatigues with POW bleached into their backs, but some Germans still wore the uniform of Rommel's Afrika Korps.

The old Case Building housed a factory which made army rainwear, the poncho kind — a rubber blanket with a head hole in the center — and regular olive drab raincoats that shed water but sweat the wearer to a fare-thee-well.

Except for Camp Norris command cars driven by corporals running errands for officers, not an automobile in Wake County was less than two years old; they had gas ration stickers on the windshields and ran on tires that were either slick or retreads. Civilians had no cuffs on their trousers. Or pleats.

1

Lawton was only another Texas town trying to win a war, if anything is ever just another something else. Which it never is. There were plenty of differences between Lawton and any other place. The forty-niners followed a trail that became the Dyersburg Road, Lawton's main street, and the gold fever was responsible for the Kentuckytown settlement from which Lawton developed. There had been a few Wake County settlers in the eighteen forties, men who always had to be farther west than anyone else. Some of the gold-seekers camped there, and then Kentuckytown became a quitting place on the California trail. It was where Pa got sick or the team died or the money ran out. It was the last campsite for those who could not make it to Sutter's. Kentuckytown was the place where a gaunt man with a worn-out woman and a wagonload of underfed young ones, after coming halfway across the continent, gave up his dream. Or settled for a lesser one.

The county's history was a long one. The old-timers and Miss Birdie Belle Ford, the permanent president of the Wake County Historical Society, claimed the McLain House occupied Jonathan Wake's campsite. Jonathan Wake was mustanging in Texas while Stephen F. Austin was still learning to walk.

The first barbed wire in the whole country was sold in the McLain House lobby, after skeptical ranchers saw demonstrations of how it would turn cows.

Later, during the depression, when every town searched for a way to bring in new people and dollars, the city fathers decided to promote Lawton's water. Old Doctor Barkley's complaint about never getting to do kidney stone operations was taken to mean that the water prevented stone formation. Signs at either end of town announced "the purist, clear, artesian water" in the nation. Lawton boosters expected a bonanza, forgetting that everyone was too poor to move away from stone-precipitating water.

Bud Riley flew his Curtiss Jenny under the Red River

bridge north of town long before the world took notice of him. The first foot-long hot dog was sold by a hole-in-the-wall cafe on Lawton's Commercial Street. Nolan Sheets wrote "The Cowhand and the Little Dogie" while he was a warehouseman at Templin's Wholesale Grocery Company. And the day Franklin Roosevelt asked for a war declaration against Japan, twenty-three survivors of the county's last Comanche raid still lived in Lawton.

Finally, Wake County was home to five generations of Tottens, descendents of the black-bearded Simeon, whose neck was broken by a hempen knot one frosty morning during the Civil War. There also lived Pages, Foxworthys, Fearses, and Wootens, whose ancestors had pitched Simeon's rope over the limb, or watched the horse driven from under him, or heard about it back in town and felt guilty, or glad.

On the fourth floor of the old courthouse Malvin Totten, in his time, hid while avoiding school. His son, George, continued the tradition, floating toilet paper scraps down the great rotunda to aggravate Foy Greer, the janitor. Foy would lumber up the stairs and go, swearing, through the unused rooms, while George hid among the discarded furniture and ballot boxes and ledgers and paintings of dead judges.

George Totten's younger brother, David, modeled himself after George, but Dave thought it a terrible waste of time to skip school only to hide out at the courthouse. Then too, in the years since George had put in his courthouse time Foy had gotten too old and arthritic for baiting him to be much fun, so he had to contend with only ordinary litter. But Foy remembered; if he saw Dave three times a day he would ask three times whether Dave's "durn brother" was still flying those "durn bummers."

David Totten was sixteen that wartime summer. It was his second year to drive a delivery truck for the Friendly Ice Company — Lucien Pemberton Blackstone, proprietor — and his world was just about to change.

3

1

Dave did not know how long he sat there trying to wake up. His mouth was dry, and the floor was cool beneath his feet. The voice came from downstairs. He opened his eyes, peered into the soft darkness, and thought of going down on an elbow for one more minute. But the voice came again. "Okay," he said, turning on the lamp. The yellow light made him weak at his stomach; he would not stay up so late again.

"David."

"Okay!" he said again, louder and with anger. His conscience stung him and he added, "Mother."

Dave heard her pad along the downstairs hallway and close her door. He popped the waistband of his jockey shorts, trying to fool himself into believing he was getting up. But he stayed put, staring at the defense savings stamps Grandma had given him Christmas. He needed to take the stamps to the post office, pay the difference, and get a war bond now that he was working full time. Otherwise, Ellis would probably stick them on a shoebox or mirror; it was a wonder he had left them alone so long. Dave had never seen anyone as sorry as Ellis.

Dave stretched and yawned but made no effort to get up. The small lamp cast a golden circle on the floor; its effect was almost hypnotic. No reasonable man could blame him if he lay back for another five minutes. He would keep both feet on the floor. Then Dave was ashamed when he remembered that it was impossible for George to stay in bed. He stood and squared his shorts. On the wall were oversized photographs of P40's and Airacobras and P38's from *Air Trails* magazine and snapshots of George and his crew with their B17.

Behind Dave were several *Esquire* Vargas and Petty girls, all heavy in the haunch, but nice; Dad objected to them, said Dave ought to have more respect for his mother and some concern for his impressionable little brother, but Dave did not agree. Mother knew women did not really look like that. And nothing had ever made an impression on Ellis.

Dave put on the blue-striped T-shirt and decided yesterday's levis would do. Starched denim, damp with sweat and ice drippings, had a smell that was satisfying to anyone short on sleep. The faint sound of music caught his attention, and Dave felt the radio he had bought when he threw the *Star-Telegram*; the dial light had burned out long ago. The top was warm. It had been on all night again. Dave wished he could blame Ellis, but he remembered turning the volume down last night while he was planning how to escape from old Shirley.

Dave held the volume control, thinking some music might help him wake up. But the only things that would be on so early were hillbilly, like "Blood on the Highway" and "Be Nobody's Darlin' But Mine"; he could not abide that. Anyway, Dad was disagreeable enough without being awakened in the middle of the night by a bunch of guitar pickers and nose pickers.

Dave switched off the radio, rolled the barbell away from the wall, and did a dozen presses. Breathing hard, he filled his pockets with the junk he had dumped out last night. He sat on his footlocker and laced the paratrooper boots, which represented most of his first week's pay on the ice route. Dave was proud yet disappointed each time he put

5

them on. Nothing was ever as satisfying as a man thought it would be when he was wanting it. Already the boots showed signs of wear; it might take two or three years, but one day they would be worn out. Having something meant starting to use it up.

The earrings old Shirley had worn last night — green rocks set in silver or something — lay on the desk. Dave had thought he wanted them when he forgot to give them back; he sometimes collected souvenirs. After they finished the watermelons, John Henry and Patsy got in the cab and he and Shirley courted up a storm on the tarpaulin in the truck bed. Dave put Shirley's earrings in his pocket so they would not be lost.

It was wrong for Dave to have the earrings; he did not think that much of Shirley. The snapshot was different; it would have been unkind not to accept that. But he should not take anything else because she kept thinking he had the sweets on her, even when he did nothing. Dave dropped the earrings into a desk drawer behind some English themes, intending to return them later. Ellis had a big curiosity about anything left out.

He tried to be quiet as he went out into the hall. Dave glanced inside George's room. The green pennant, the framed photographs, the trophies, the cowboy boots in the closet were as George had left them. A pocked, soapy marble at the foot of the bed meant Ellis had been prowling around in there again. Dave closed the door. One day Ellis was going to get his tail kicked up between his shoulder blades.

The faded maroon rug muffled his steps. Dinty, George's old brindle bulldog. lay in Ellis' doorway with his head between his paws. He rolled his eyes and wagged his stub of a tail. Dave bent and patted him. Dinty did not move but his pink tongue covered his nose for an instant. Dave went on, feeling bad. With George overseas, Dinty did not get the attention he needed. Ellis was no company at all.

Dinty always slept in the wicker chair next to George's

bed. For a long time after George left he used the chair, but finally he settled for the floor in Ellis' room. Lying in the doorway with his head on the edge of the hall rug he would know if anyone passed.

Dave eased down the stairs and into the bathroom. He waited for the fluorescent tube over the medicine cabinet to stop flickering. Ellis had mashed the toothpaste in the middle and left the cap off again. He was too old for that; Dad ought to be harder on him.

Dave filled the basin with cold water and held his face under. He dripped water as he tried to decide what to put on his hair, the Rose Brilliantine — ten cents a gallon at Kresses, weak red and sweet smelling — or the good stuff George left behind when he was home on leave. George's stuff did not make hair comb any better, but every hillbilly at West's cafe, every farmer hunkered at the Jonathan Wake statue on the square, every cowhand at the mule barn, used Kresses hair grease. On a Saturday night the pool hall smelled as if a jug of Rose Brilliantine had been busted on the stove. Dave used some of George's stuff and started for the kitchen, scattering drops of water each time he ran the comb through his wet hair. He felt better, but he resolved to go to bed earlier.

His mother's voice, coming from her room, startled him. "Do you want breakfast?"

"Nome. I'm running late." The back door was open. Light from the coming dawn reflected in the wet spots on the floor.

He turned on the light in the kitchen, a big room, pine panelled on two sides and papered on the others. Sometimes at breakfast, sitting on a chrome-legged stool, he studied the shapes in the red and black and green wallpaper, but usually when he did that he was late to work and dragged through the day as if he were asleep.

One morning Dave was chewing a gristly piece of steak and reading a Kellogg's Corn Flakes box when he decided there was a wolf head in the wallpaper. He went completely

7

to sleep and did not wake up until he banged his head on the wall. He glanced about, embarrassed, afraid someone had seen him, although he knew nobody else was up. He thought maybe he had hypnotized himself.

Fortunately, George had bought from Johnson and Smith Company a book called *Mesmerism Made Easy* by Professor Edward Shapiro. It was a best seller. Every month there was a picture of Professor Shapiro on the back cover of *Action Comics* holding the book out and promising readers command over friends, business associates, and other executives. Albert Briggs, who had read the book, said he could put the make on any girl in Lawton if he wanted to, but he did not want to.

Once Dave came in from the ice route feeling as if he had been in a dream all day. He had forgotten to deliver half a dozen customers and had stabbed Mrs. Creighton Allen's butter with his ice pick. Dave went into George's room, and sat down in the wicker chair with *Mesmerism Made Easy*. He read the chapter on self-hypnosis half a dozen times, but Professor Shapiro did not even mention wallpaper.

Dave opened the Frigidaire and felt its cool breath on his face. Since pork was off the ration list now, Mother had bought a good-looking ham. But ham sandwiches gave him heartburn when he had not slept enough. Some hamburger patties remained from last night. The grease on top could be scraped off, or he could melt it in a skillet. Either way was too much trouble; Dave ate one of the patties cold and shuddered as the grease stuck to the roof of his mouth. He reached for the other, then thought better of it. A sour pickle cut the grease pretty well, and a piece of cherry pie made him almost forget the hamburger.

Outside the sky over Mrs. Steele's house was getting lighter. A car went past, its tires making a heavy, humming sound on the red brick pavement. Somebody had new retreads.

Dave got out a quart of milk and the can of chocolate

syrup; it had been opened by Ellis, which was apparent from the bait-can cut, a half moon in the top bent up to form a handle. Dave shook the milk bottle until the cream disappeared. He worked his tongue against the roof of his mouth wishing he had left the hamburger alone. He drank the milk down about four fingers, as Shy would say, added chocolate syrup, and replaced the stopper. He made sure his ice pick and scabbard were in place, switched off the light, and went out the back door.

Dave stopped on the small porch, glad to be awake when everyone else was asleep. The stillness and gentleness of the Texas morning lifted him up and at the same time made him sad. He felt he knew something then that he had not known before, but if he tried to tell it, he could not.

Across the street to the north was the holy roller church. In back of Dave's house was old lady Steele's garden and chicken yard; lots of baseballs and footballs had been lost there. Someone would start to shinny over her fence to get a ball and she would come running, mopping at her flushed forehead with an apron. Sometimes she threw the ball back, but usually she took it inside as she threatened to call the laws. Once Isaac Bates cursed Mrs. Steele for keeping his football; Dad whipped Dave for just being there.

On the south was the vacant lot where George's friends used to meet. Dave had played football and rubber guns and capture-the-flag there, but the lot had fallen on evil times. Ellis and his crew had built, from packing crates, cardboard, tarpaper, and other trash, something they called a tree house, although the whole mess sat flat on the ground. Dave had told Ellis not to locate the tree house in the center where it ruined the lot for anything else, but Ellis got snotty and put it there anyway. Dave would have hit him, except that it would have meant trouble with Dad.

Now Ellis and his friends had a hard time playing baseball on the lot. Hits through the pitcher's box usually went inside the tree house. By the time the fielder went in, found

9

the ball, came out, and made his throw, all the runners were home safe. In a football game most passes had to be thrown over the tree house, but not one of that crew — Ellis, Reedy, Otho, or T.A. — had enough arm to clear the roof without the ball taking at least one bounce.

Dr. Barkley, whose father caused the kidney stone myth, lived south of the lot. Wind blew Ellis' litter into his yard, and Dad was always over there picking candy wrappers out of the flower beds. Dad would come home, red-faced and angry, and tell Ellis he intended to put the whole damned lot into a Victory garden.

Dave was pleased with his part of the world. He took a deep breath and held it. Everything around him was quiet and peaceful; he could not believe that men were fighting in Italy and on a dozen Pacific islands on such a morning, that George might be flying a mission right then.

Dave sucked in his gut and, holding the bottle bartender-style, he went down the steps and across the yard. His boots made dark tracks in the wet grass. He shook the bottle with some apprehension; he had drunk lots of slightly colored milk on sleepy mornings when he misjudged the chocolate syrup. Dave pulled the stopper and threw it into the doctor's front yard. If anyone noticed, Ellis would get the blame.

Dave took a long pull on the bottle. He had seen movies and photographs of lots of places. Someday he would travel to Hollywood, New York, London, Paris, but Lawton was the only place for him. George felt the same way, although he had never said so. Dave used to worry about George not wanting to come back to Lawton. Grady Hemphill, of Grady's Cleaners, always said you could not keep them down on the farm after they had seen Paree. Grady said French women were mighty good looking, and he knew since he had been gassed in World War I. One of Dave's favorite stories in *Flying Aces* magazine was about an American aviator who was going to stay in London, England, because it had more culture than the U.S.A.

10

One day when Dave's uneasiness got too much for him, he asked Grandpa what would happen after George saw Paree. Grandpa snorted and said George would do what Grady Hemphill did. He said that once Grady inhaled enough mustard gas to get out of the army his shirttail did not hit his rear until he was back in Wake County, which made Dave feel better. The *Flying Aces* hero had the sweets on a London girl and anyway he was basically a Yankee, which was the same as not having anyplace to come home to anyhow. George always wrote that he was in a hurry to get back, and he loved Mary, and she would never leave Lawton.

The Friendly Ice Company was only four blocks from home, a quart of chocolate milk away. Dave checked the bottle level and slowed down. If he got to the plant too fast he had to chug-a-lug the chocolate milk. He surveyed the disarray of the wagon yard — Dave never understood how it made any money — and read the Calvary Baptist Church display board. Calvary was not Lawton's main bunch of Baptists; it was a hardshell, or maybe a softshell, church; Dave was not sure which. They either did or did not belong to the Southern Baptist Convention, and they did or did not send missionaries to Africa. Or they all took communion from the same cup, or washed one another's feet, or sprinkled instead of baptized or had some other odd practice. Anyhow, Calvary was different from the First Baptist, where Dave belonged. There was always an ad in the Saturday *Caller-Times* about Calvary's Sunday services. The sermon titles were always unsettling, and the preacher looked as if he could take the hide right off a confirmed sinner.

Mrs. Bridges lived next to Calvary Baptist. She had more stars in her window flag than anyone else in Lawton. When Dave enlisted Mother would have two stars, but he was not going anywhere until he was at least seventeen, which was six months away. Dave left the curb and walked down the middle of the street. It made him feel powerful and impor-

11

tant. He was six feet tall, weighed 200 pounds, was a Lawton Lions guard and a full-fledged Friendly iceman. His people had been in Wake County forever. His father's name was scrawled across the side of Gumpert's Market; well-weathered, it still read "Malvin Totten plus" someone who had been scratched out. Dave always wondered if Mother's name had been written there, but he never had the nerve to ask.

The sun was rising somewhere in Texas. Up ahead Dave saw the outline of the great Friendly plant. He finished the chocolate milk and increased his speed. The boots made a good, solid, heavy sound. He pitched the bottle up, caught it, tucked it under his arm, ran a few yards, sidestepped several tacklers, and sprinted for the goal line at the Cities Service station's green pumps. Dave dropped into a fast walk. Later he would trade the bottle for an RC or a Nehi orange.

When Dave reached the Friendly parking lot he found John Henry standing in the bed of his ice truck. John Henry was tall and slender and had straight, brown hair.

"Morning, Slicker," Dave said.

"Don't Slicker me," John Henry snapped, disappearing behind the sideboards which bore the Friendly name, phone number, and two painted arms shaking hands. He raised up and threw a chunk of watermelon rind that barely missed Dave and splattered against the plant wall below the V-for-Victory sign.

Dave's laugh caught in his throat as he realized that the damning evidence had been there all night, proof positive that he and the slicker had violated the rule against skylarking around with girls in Friendly trucks and that they had cut — and if not wholly consumed, had, at least destroyed — seven Friendly watermelons. Dave was stunned.

"Didn't clean it up, didja? Dumb bastard." John Henry threw again.

Dave dodged, but the rind grazed his shoulder. "Cut it

out, Slicker." He set the bottle down and ran around to the back of the 1940 Plymouth. He groaned. "It's all still here."

"No, the tooth fairy took them and left you a quarter." He swung, but Dave backed out of reach.

"Okay, John Henry, I'll haul you out of there, and we'll get really crossways, and Daddy Warbucks will find out the whole business."

John Henry glowered, then got busy bringing the rinds to the tailgate. Dave took several to the trash barrel, holding them away from his body so the sticky juice missed his boots. He hurried back for more, grateful that they had gotten there before Mr. Blackstone. John Henry was sweeping the dried black seeds off the heavy, quilted tarpaulin. Dave was relieved as he took the last rind to the rusted-out oil drum.

Daddy Warbucks, a title held by Mr. Blackstone because of his stinginess and a tie pin with a glass head almost as big as a marble, had been cool toward Dave ever since he took the door off his truck. Dave was uneasy; a man needed to keep his misdeeds clearly in mind in case he had to answer on short notice, but lately Dave's conscience had gotten so hardened he could not remember details.

It was still too early, and Dave was too recently awake, for so much excitement. His hands were sticky with watermelon juice, and he was sweating. He was just about fed up with John Henry, whose blame was greater than Dave's since his truck was the one involved. Dave wiped his hands on the canvas crushed-ice bag hanging from the sideboard. A dried watermelon seed was stuck inside his forearm; he flipped it onto the tarpaulin where his friend was sweeping.

John Henry kept criticizing Dave as he tried to dislodge, with the frayed, yellow-handled broom, a few seeds which were stuck to the tarp. Suddenly Dave yelled, "Shut your face. If you would eat anything but hearts we would have had just one watermelon, not seven, back here. Besides, it's your truck."

"Yeah, but who got the benefits? I had to stay up front

13

and drive." John Henry broke into a grin. "I never did see any passengers' heads in the mirror." He jumped to the ground and swung at Dave with the soggy broom.

Dave took the blow on his side. As he jerked the broom away from John Henry, a batch of straw fell out; nobody had made anything right since the war began. "Cut it out," Dave said. "I'm not woke up yet."

"Hey, old Shirley has got the hots for you."

Dave grunted. He pitched the broom onto the back dock and retrieved his milk bottle. He could still smell the watermelon; he noticed, with regret, a wet place on his levis where the juice had dripped.

In the east the sky was yellow-streaked. John Henry ground his starter, bringing Dave out of his reverie. "Hold on. I may need a shove." Dave jumped into the orange Ford through the cavity left by removal of the door. His motor turned over, then quit. He motioned for the slicker to wait. John Henry gunned his engine and acted put upon. Dave tried again, successfully. The cab filled with fumes and smoke.

John Henry's Plymouth lurched, stopped, and lurched again, as he mismanaged the clutch. He whipped the pickup around, scattering gravel, and sped past the corner of the plant.

Dave, appalled by his friend's driving, eased around the building with his foot out on the running board and backed up to the dock. He vaulted onto the damp concrete platform that extended across the front of the plant. To Dave's right, just past the ice vault, steps led down from the dock to ground level in front of the office. Cedric Cooper, the plant manager, stood there, scratching his back against the door jamb and watching Dave and John Henry. As usual, his hands were stuffed deep into the pockets of his khakis; a chewed match dangled from his mouth, and there was a smirk on his leathery face. He said, "Sunday School must of let out."

Dave smiled, but remained wary. Cedric was crafty;

14

ordinarily he paid no attention to them until the routes were run. It was too early for people to be as happy as Cedric seemed. The soft, sweet watermelon smell and lack of sleep were making Dave queasy. He reviewed his recent misdeeds.

John Henry was puzzling over a route note he had written himself yesterday. Dave glanced at the message; Ellis could write better than that. Cedric sauntered up onto the dock, leaned against the yellow brick, and crossed his legs, smirking. He had chewed the end of the match to a frazzle and was regularly spitting wood. Dave ignored him.

John Henry shrugged, wadded up the note, and threw it onto the apron. He started bragging to Cedric about something he claimed to have done, some exceptional service he had rendered to a customer. Dave barely listened, knowing whatever John Henry said he had done would have been commendable if he had really done it. But he hadn't.

Cedric's smirk widened.

"Let's load you up first, Slicker," Dave said, anxious to get away from Cedric.

John Henry ignored him. "Like I say, Ced, some guys just do their job, but I figure if you gonna work for somebody, then give your whole might and main." He dropped his eyes, moved by the sudden recognition of his deep dedication, and swallowed hard. John Henry hung his hooks on the sideboard and draped the heavy tarp over his cab before enlarging upon the good deed he had done. "And Ced, I bet I put a hundred or a hundred and fifty in that house every day from now on. I just did my duty as I saw it, but that lady thought it was something special."

Dave tried not to look at Cedric, whose smirk kept setting in deeper all the time. The plant manager chuckled meanly every once in awhile, a sign John Henry stupidly interpreted as appreciation.

Dave smoothed John Henry's tarp and gazed up and down Kentuckytown Avenue, staying clear of Cedric. When there was nothing to do but turn around he grabbed his

15

hooks and hurried past Cedric. He opened the vault door and the cold air hit him like a hammer. He hesitated, storing some of the morning's warmth before going inside.

John Henry followed Dave, saying, "Oh Lord, it was great, Ced. I might even put two fifty or three hundred a day in there." He illustrated his points with exaggerated hand and arm gestures.

Cedric gave an evil cackle, making chill bumps stand out on Dave's arms. Suddenly Cedric's high good humor was no longer tolerable. Dave demanded, "What's on your stupid mind, Cedric?"

"Oh, nothing." Cedric began humming "La Golondrina", the world's worst song. "Not one single thing."

John Henry was peeved by the interruption.

Dave felt like hitting either or both of them; he believed everyone should have the basic decency to leave everyone else alone until everyone was good and awake.

John Henry, oblivious to Cedric's behavior, struggled with the three hundred pound blocks, getting them ready to be tipped over. The plant manager had gone to the other side of the vault and was putting twenty-fives on the ramp so they would slide out the little door onto the dock when the lever was pulled. Dave started to warn John Henry about Cedric, but the slicker said, "The reason you are such a son-of-a-bitch in the mornings, David, is because you don't get up early like I do and read the paper and hear the latest news and all."

"Hell, you listen to hillbilly music and look at the funnies and make your mother get up and cook you breakfast. That's all you do."

"If we hadn't been friends since I was seven and you were six I wouldn't want nothing to do with you because of your disposition."

Dave lowered his voice. "Cedric is up to something."

"Who?" John Henry was too light to be a good iceman; he was tugging at a block without the slightest success.

"That sneaky bastard," Dave nodded toward the manager. "And keep your voice down."

"Aw." The slicker strained against the block.

"He's over there grinning and humming."

"Dave, I hummed all morning until I saw how you left the watermelon rinds in my truck."

"He laughs, too, every once in awhile. And chews on that matchstick."

John Henry's eyes were cold. "You ain't tolerant."

"Okay, knothead, but I told you." Dave threw his hooks into a three hundred pounder and brought it over.

"Hey, Ced," John Henry called, "when I first saw this customer . . . ."

"Oh shut up," Dave told him. As he snaked the ice toward the door, Dave heard Cedric go, "Hee, hee, hee."

While they put seven of the three hundred pounders on his truck, John Henry tried to breathe new life into his story. Daddy Warbucks shot out of the office, a bicycle clip holding the faded blue trousers close about his skinny calf.

"Hi, Mr. Blackstone," John Henry said.

The old man did not answer. He frowned at them. Then, abruptly, he went back inside.

"Slicker, why don't you tell Daddy Warbucks that crap about your good deeds?" Dave asked. "Then maybe he would speak to you."

John Henry glared at the old man's bicycle, which was leaned against the machinery room door. "You work your heart out bending over backwards to build good will for the company. Then your boss don't even say good morning, which is a fine howdy do. It is enough to make you half do your job and let the business go to the dogs."

"He's got them blue pants on again," Dave observed.

Cedric snickered and bit down on a fresh match.

"One day I am going to jump on Daddy Warbucks' bicycle and hit every chug hole in town." John Henry's hands shook as he combed his hair.

The three Friendly employees fell silent; one was convinced that something bad was going to happen, one amused himself with treacherous thoughts, and the other, except for being snubbed by his employer, at peace with the world. Across the street, Mr. Smalley, wearing a folded-down paper sack on his head, swept the sidewalk in front of his store. His younger son was a fighter pilot in England, where George was. The other boy had been in the Royal Air Force before Pearl Harbor; after his death the government paid Mrs. Smalley's fare to Washington so Lord Halifax could present her son's medals.

Cedric laughed out loud. He had substituted a homemade cigarette for his matchstick. Dave wondered if the manager knew his son, Warren, rolled his own, too. Cedric cleared his throat and said, "I seen something real funny last night."

Dave froze, but John Henry's eyes were bright and his face eager. "What was that?"

"Two young punks and a couple of gals. In a ice truck they were, blaring out South Summit like a bat out of Hell." Cedric cackled and slapped his skinny thigh.

John Henry's eyes got big and his face went white.

Dave sucked air. He tried to laugh, but nothing came out. "That must have been funny, all right," he said.

"And I bet that truck was full of Friendly watermelons." Cedric's cackle became a high-pitched wheeze.

"For Pete's sake, Cedric," John Henry pleaded, motioning toward the office. "He's gonna hear." John Henry opened the vault door, and Dave dragged the limp plant manager inside.

Dave was scared. If Daddy Warbucks got suspicious and came barrelling in, Cedric would be too dim-witted to come up with a good lie. Cedric was collapsed against the wall. Suddenly it was funny to Dave, too, especially the slicker's expression; he looked as if a truck had backed over his foot.

"Your buddy there," Cedric pointed at John Henry. "was

all scrooched down in the cab so nobody could see him. And the redhead was giving him emergency treatment."

Dave guffawed.

"I'm gonna go count the watermelons." Cedric wiped his eyes and pounded Dave on the back to help with his breathing.

"We'd better get you loaded, Dave." John Henry was trying to look pitiful. He paced the vault with his hands outstretched helplessly. Every time Dave was about to stop laughing he would look at Cedric, and they would start over.

"I am just gonna leave," John Henry threatened, deciding to be angry. "I don't have to help you. The only reason I do is because. . . . "

Just then the door was flung open, and Lucien Pemberton Blackstone's rectangular face appeared. Suddenly, the three Friendly employees were sobered and busy.

"Hi, Mr. Blackstone," John Henry said. He threw his hooks into a block as Dave caught it from the other side. Dave jerked it toward him; the movement caught John Henry off balance and he sprawled across the wet floor.

"Workmen's compensation does not cover horseplay," Daddy Warbucks declared, staring at John Henry's damp shirt and trousers. He tied a twenty-five pounder with binder twine and left.

Dave's truck was soon loaded. Fortunately he had his change and record sheet, but John Henry had to go to the office to get his. When he came out John Henry's hands shook as he stuffed the change money into his pockets. "That old bastard," he said.

"What did he say?" Dave asked.

"About what?"

"Anything."

"That he knew a guy who got hurt horseplayin and he didn't get any workman's compensation, and that I been putting too much brake fluid in my truck, and I couldn't put in anymore for awhile." John Henry looked balefully

19

at the Blackstone bicycle. "He don't never even speak to me except when he's got something hard to say."

Dave was relieved. "Well, Slicker, there's a war on. Brake fluid is scarce."

"I can't hardly get my truck stopped empty, much less loaded."

"Drag your foot."

"Very funny. Ha. Ha."

"Use your reverse."

"I do. I can practically feel the gear teeth grinding off." John Henry retreated within himself, then stated, "You work your tail to the bone giving good service and you get fifty pound customers to go up to three hundred."

Dave flinched. Someday John Henry was going to get so caught up in his lies that he would not be able to come back to reality.

"But if faulty company equipment makes me kill somebody, I will be able to live with myself." John Henry's face was appropriately long. "It will be on Mr. Blackstone's head."

"You probably wouldn't kill them." Dave squeezed the slicker's shoulder sympathetically.

"Well, I'm gonna try not to."

"Just break a few bones. Skin them up some." Dave laughed. "Maybe drag them a few hundred feet."

"You are a son-of-a-bitch, David. I will not ever discuss anything serious with you from now on."

Cedric came out of the vault with his clipboard, smirking. "Think I better take me a little watermelon inventory," he said.

Dave swung into his truck; a ton of ice made her set low in spite of heavy-duty springs. Dave had taken off the door — in spite of Mr. Blackstone's protests — so he could almost fall into the cab.

John Henry came to the side of Dave's truck admiring the doorless cab. "Soon as I get through today, I'm gonna take my door off."

"You said that yesterday."

"Well, I'm going to."

"And last week and the week before that."

"See if I don't." John Henry glanced toward the water-melon room and lowered his voice. "But maybe I better wait till things ease off."

Dave stuck his foot outside the cab and tapped a tattoo on the running board with the trooper's boot.

"Daddy Warbucks might check the melon vault. . . . "

Dave waved him off. He pulled away from the dock and turned onto Kentuckytown Avenue. He took a deep breath and sucked in his gut. The ice pick scabbard at his side made him feel especially fit, like Johnny Mack Brown and Bob Steele and the others he used to see at the Saturday foot-and-onion show. He imagined himself as Errol Flynn playing a pirate captain and sword fighting in black long johns. The truck moved like a Spanish galleon, with a heavy, powerful directness. He waved at a street sweeper and vowed to see what the encyclopedia said a piece-of-eight was worth and where the Dry Tortugas were located.

Dave glanced at the paratrooper boot marking time on the running board. "Oh, she rolls along like a cannonball," he sang into the stillness of the new morning.

2

The load was half gone and he had worked up a sweat
by the time he got to the A & P. The stiff levis had accommodated themselves to him, and the T-shirt was stuck to
his back. He took in three one hundred pound blocks, picked
up a sack of sugar, and counted a dozen eggs into a brown
bag. Mrs. Eddie Blevins was arguing with the cashier
about the price of something. Dave loitered by the Rice
Krispies, where she could not see him. Mrs. Eddie Blevins
knew everything that happened in Lawton, never forgot any
of it, and told all she remembered and suspected.

Dave waited until Mrs. Blevins was gone, then paid for
his groceries. He would have to bring the sugar ration
stamps tomorrow; the best thing about a small town was
that people trusted each other. Of course, small towns had
bad points, too, such as Mrs. Eddie Blevins. When Dave
came out of the store she was leaning inside her green
Chrysler fanning out the heat with a newspaper.

Dave went east on the Dyersburg Road past the post
office and across the railroad tracks. A couple of blocks
before Pendleton Street he started slowing; his brakes
were as bad as John Henry's. He made a wide, easy turn,
which barely disturbed the load. Pendleton was two lanes
of hot-top and heavy gravel shoulders, lined with mulberry
trees, vegetable gardens, and porch swings.

Dave stopped before a small white frame house and made sure the back of the window ice card was to the street. Dave set what was left of the emergency brake and got out, deciding that leaving the motor running would make less racket than starting it again. Dave picked up the *Star-Tele-gram* as he crossed the yard, left it behind the screen door with the sugar and eggs, and ran back to the truck. He glanced up and down the street to see if anyone had noticed him, and headed for town.

At Harry's Farm Store, Dave iced the Coke boxes and water fountain. He was always impressed by the dank smell of grain and feed in the huge building; it held enough merchandise to stock a dozen stores. Flour, in forty-eight and ninety-six pound colored bags, was stacked as high as a tall man could reach beneath a sign reading "Colorful Cambric Flour — Eat the flour. Wear the sack. If not satisfied, your money back." Dave made his New McLain House delivery and got rid of the rest of the load — except for one fifty — at the Lone Star Cafe, where in three chances on the punchboard he did not win the long-barrelled flashlight. He took his time as he went back out Dyersburg. Some men he did not know were working on Lawton Drug's neon sign. Before the war everybody had been acquainted with everybody, but lots of new people had come to open businesses and to build and run the army camp. He coasted up to the red light at the square. Speedy Thomas had stopped a red-faced young ensign, probably for speeding. The Navy officer stood in front of the Lyric Theater with his shoulders drooping. The woman passenger looked as if she had not been getting enough sleep.

Dave was watching the rearview mirror to see if Speedy wrote a ticket for the sailor; he was almost upon the railroad tracks when he remembered his business. He stepped on the gas — crossing slowly was not manly — and hit the rails too hard; the empty truck bounced a foot into the air, and Dave banged his head on the ceiling. He stomped the brake pedal, which went clear to the floorboard without effect. His hooks and shoulder pad had not come off the sideboard post, but Dave's forehead smarted where it had been scraped by the sun visor.

Dave turned off Dyersburg a block west of Pendleton. He circled the block before stopping in the gravel driveway of the white house. No one was out in any of the yards. The sun shone through a cloudless sky, and the heat was beginning to build. Carrying the fifty, Dave stepped onto the porch.

The screen was still ajar; the untouched groceries meant she was not yet awake. Disappointed, Dave kicked the paper inside and picked up the sugar and eggs. Halfway down the dark hall he stopped at the bedroom. A sliver of sunlight came through the torn shade and fell upon the throat of a sleeping woman. Dave went on back to the kitchen and put the eggs and sugar on the table. He raised the lid and eased the ice into the box. He started to wipe his wet hands on the levis, then noticed a monogrammed tea towel; he held it to his face before blotting his hands. Unwashed dishes filled the sink, and ironing was heaped on the drainboard.

Dave went back to the bedroom. The woman lay on her side with her back to him and a foot sticking out from under the sheet. Her black hair spread over the pillow. Dave stepped around a chair piled high with clothes and movie magazines and sat down on the bed. He touched her waist; she stirred and covered his hand with her own.

"You sleepy?" he asked. His voice always sounded softer, wiser, older when he talked to her.

"Uh huh." She smiled but did not open her eyes. Dave kissed her cheek and throat. In a single graceful movement she rolled over, put her slender arms around his neck, and pulled him to her. "What time is it?"

"Late." Dave kissed her softly, then harder as her arms tightened. "And I'm hungry."

She started to get up, but he stopped her. "You want me to come back later?"

"No, honey, turn on the stove. I'll be in."

Dave went back to the kitchen, stuck a match to a burner, got out the skillet, and untwisted the neck of the egg sack. She came in wearing a faded blue chenille bathrobe tied at her waist with a frayed cord. She took the egg he was about to break and pushed him aside.

"You want me to do anything?"

"Just talk to me." She broke the eggs and threw the shells into a cardboard box beneath the sink. She knelt and opened the icebox door. Dave sat at the table, leaning on his elbows and marvelling at her grace. Women did not usually look like much in the morning, but she was beautiful. He wished George knew about her. But he could not ever discuss her with anyone. He hated to think of her being married to someone else. Dave put his feet up in the other chair.

She pushed the hair off her forehead and raked the eggs into the plates. "Do you want bacon?"

"Nope."

She set the table and used a knife to extract the toast from the broken toaster. Dave caught her waist and turned her to him. He stood and put his arms around her. "Hazel, do you love him?"

She stiffened but did not try to move.

"Ted, I mean."

"I know who you mean," Hazel snapped. She pushed, as if to get away, but did not resist when he pulled her closer. She gazed into his face, then past him. "I don't think about it."

"Lots of times I wish I could take you places, maybe go to Dallas and dance some. Or like that." When she did not answer he added, "I never danced in Dallas but I would like to with you."

She leaned her head on his shoulder. "He was stationed there. And they were transferring him here, so he asked me to marry him."

Dave kissed her, and she clung to him. "You're sweaty," she said, but when he backed away she added, "I like it."

25

"Hazel?"

She raised her eyes.

"If I was old enough, I'd make you leave him and marry me."

She pressed two fingers to his lips, then slipped away. Dave held her chair as she sat down. One of Ted's combat boots lay near the table; its rough upper was thick with brown dubbing. Dave kicked and the boot skidded into the hall. He swung his leg over the back of his chair. "I ain't old enough to do a damn thing," he complained, glaring at the boot. "I don't even have a driver's license."

Hazel put her hand on his clenched fist. When she leaned forward the robe fell away from her breasts. "It's hard being a certain age."

"You ain't much older," he charged. "Eighteen. Nineteen."

She smiled sadly.

"You ain't hardly any older," he repeated, gently this time.

"I'm a little bit," she agreed and squeezed his hand.

Shy, John Henry, and O.P. had each taken out their second loads when Dave got back. Cedric, still smirking, helped him get the ice on the truck, something he had never done before. "You ain't gonna tell Daddy Warbucks about last night? Are you?"

"Something happen last night?" Cedric had deep laugh wrinkles. His skin was thick and brown enough to prove he had done his share of plowing and cotton chopping. "If anything happened involving Friendly rolling stock and watermelons I would purt near have to tell that fine old gentleman. Don't you think so?"

Dave was still trying to devise a threat to use against Cedric when he left the plant, but his thoughts were mainly of Hazel, her beauty, how it was to hold her, the flowers

26

she always had in the fruit jar on the table, and how lost she was to him because of a few years. He had never met Ted, but Dave did not like him at all.

Dave had half a dozen stops near the army camp, Ma and Pa grocery stores and filling stations that sold cheap East Texas gasoline. He remembered when Camp Norris was just good farmland. Now, in addition to the soldiers, fifteen thousand German and Italian prisoners of war were interned there. They kept breaking out, twenty or thirty at a time. They were reconciled to being out of the war; they only wanted to see a little of the country. Someone painted "Slow, Prisoners Escaping" on the military reservation sign.

The roundhouse was the last stop on his third load. Dave always looked forward to it. The huge red, heavy-timbered, old barn smelled of dead steam, and grease, and wood smoke, and coal smoke, and oil smoke. Dave lowered a hundred and fifty pounds into each water barrel and chipped off the tops of the blocks until the lids fit. He took the ice book from the nail back of the trainmaster's roll-top desk in the yard office and tore out coupons for the delivery. Dave thought about seeing what the overhauling crews were doing, but he was running late because of the time with Hazel; that was always the fastest part of the day. Albert Hook's dad, coming out of the machine shop, waved, and Dave returned his greeting. He stopped to watch a locomotive being driven onto the turntable. The engineer hung out of the cab window following the directions of the brakeman, who bent down to see that the tracks met. The locomotive sounded terribly reluctant about moving; then there was the grinding of steel on steel as the engine began rolling, and the clanking as each set of wheels dropped onto the tracks on the table. As the tender passed, the brakeman straightened and caught onto the ladder. At the same time, the fireman was clambering down from the cab; he wiped his face with a red bandana, and after the locomotive's brakes were set he started the gasoline motor. Dave leaned, giving some body english, as the turntable shuddered into motion. The tiny motor, coughing regularly, was making the table revolve, changing the direction of the tracks on which the mighty steam-engine sat. Dave experienced that same awe locomotives had aroused in him since before he flattened his first penny on a railroad track.

The engineer shouted to him. Dave could not tell who it was, but everyone at the roundhouse knew him; Grandpa used to take him aboard the locomotives in spite of the rules. The little motor was slowing down. The fireman stopped the table so its tracks met one of the dozen sets that came to the edge of the great round hole. The brake-man, standing beside the cowcatcher now, motioned and the locomotive rolled off the table, as the fireman climbed toward the cab.

Dave started the truck. He wished he could ride the turntable again, but he was too old to ask anyone and too old for anyone to think he might be interested. He and George might hire out on the railroad one day. After the war Henry Kaiser was going to make cars that would sell for four hundred dollars; they might even buy six or seven and start a taxi company. It was hard to make plans since George might want to go to college or do any number of other things. Whatever, he and George would be together.

Dave drove under the rusty steel arch and turned onto the narrow road. He fought the steering wheel, avoiding the deepest ruts where he was liable to hit high center and ruin an oil pan. He was thinking about Hazel when he saw a stooped man in faded blue overalls and jumper trudging along the road. Dave hit the brakes, which did not slow him at all. He felt foolish as he passed by, stomping the pedal again and again. The truck coasted to a stop and Dave leaned across the seat and held the door open while the old man caught up.

"Grandpa," Dave said in greeting.

The old man's broad smile and gold tooth made him

look almost as young as Dad. Breathing hard from catching up, he put his scarred, black lunch box on the floor and got in. "You about through for the day?"

"No sir, I got two more loads and they'll be special orders this afternoon."

"I seen a lots better brakes on trucks."

"Yes sir. I was thinking about putting in some brake fluid." Dave stuck his foot out on the running board, then thought better of it and brought all his members inside.

"By golly, you took your door off," Grandpa said, amused.

"I can get in and out easier, deliver half again as much ice." Dave liked being around Grandpa, probably because he always approved of what Dave did. Better, Grandpa always noticed.

"I can see how you would." Grandpa had a thin-edged laugh that made others want to laugh, too.

Usually Dave tried to see what the truck would do as he dodged the high centers of the roundhouse road, but now he drove with extra care, not wanting to demonstrate his braking power again. Grandpa had been on his side in the uproar about the iceman's job; Dad had said a fifteen year old boy — he never got anybody's age right — had no business driving a truck. It made no difference that Dave had run the same route, after they had the same argument, last summer. Nor did it help that he drove the cleaning truck after school all last year. The main problem was that Dad had assumed he was going to ask to use the family car.

Grandpa had finally got Dad straightened out; after all his bucking, and snorting, and pitching, and yelling, Grandpa just gave Dad that steady look. Grandpa had the Indian sign on him. Dad still complained that Dave was going to run somebody over and he would be the one sued and stated that his father had no business interfering with his kids. But the trouble was over.

"Your mother all right?"

"Yes sir."

"And Ellis?"

"Fine, sir."

"You like your job?"

"Yes sir, Grandpa."

Grandpa's face was broad and strong beneath the faded blue cap. The gold tooth caught the light when he talked. He stretched his arm along the seat back and rested his hand on Dave's shoulder. "You might turn out to be a pretty fair ball player."

"Yes sir, if I don't go in the army."

"Maybe the war will be over soon. Henry Ford said it couldn't last more than two months." Grandpa sighed. "But it was four months ago when he said that."

They did not talk much after that. Dave kept still so Grandpa would not move his hand. He remembered when George made Eagle Scout. Grandpa, dressed up with his watch chain across his vest, brought George a barely weaned pup that they called Dinty after the character in *Maggie and Jiggs*. Even Dave could tell Grandpa had been drinking. While Dave and George played with the pup and Mother watched with a dishrag in her hand, Dad shouted that, by God, when his kids needed a dog he would get them one. Then Dinty waddled over to the playpen where Ellis sat enthralled and confirmed Dad's fears by puddling on the linoleum.

Everybody laughed. Finally Dad did, too. Ellis caught the spirit and fell over and banged his head on the playpen and cried, and Dad remembered he was angry and said it was hard enough to raise a houseful of boys without meddlers. He insisted on driving Grandpa home, and when he got back he smelled a lot like Grandpa had.

Dave stopped at a red brick house with cannas bordering the sidewalk. Grandpa cleared his throat and squeezed Dave's shoulder and said, "It was a good idea, taking the door off." He ambled across the yard, carrying the black lunch box and looking old. He picked up a piece of tree limb and pitched it into the driveway. He waited at the front door; Dave knew he would have to drive away before Grandpa would go inside. One day, Dave thought, somebody like Hazel would love him, and he wanted her to know Grandpa. Dave eased away from the curb and kept his speed down until he was out of sight.

———————

Ace Howard's Acme Ice Company truck was parked in front of the junior high school, which seemed to be an evil omen. Dave had never met Ace, but he knew Ace's reputation with girls. Ace had a Clark Gable moustache and long black hair. Old man Carson, who bootlegged whiskey out of the back of his drugstore, was always talking about Ace's sexual exploits. No doubt Ace got lots of girls drunk on bootleg whiskey and took advantage of them. Dave hoped Ace would never meet Hazel.

Ace's route was clear across town from Dave's, so there was little chance of his running into Hazel. But if he did, what real danger was there? First off, it was Dave that Hazel was crazy about. Secondly, he was bigger and better built than Ace. Third, he probably was as good looking, not counting moustaches. And he could probably whip Ace. But there was always this: Ace was twenty-three or so and had won the Purple Heart in the Pacific, and Dave was sixteen and had been no further from home than Fort Worth. He disliked Ace more than he did Ted. At least, Ted had married Hazel and was not ruining the life of every girl in Wake County.

After two more loads the route was finished. Big sweat circles stained Dave's T-shirt, and the levis, damp with ice drippings, stuck to his legs. Cedric was straightening the soft drink crates on the back dock when Dave parked.

"Where's the slicker, Ced?"

"Talking to the watermelons."

Dave got back to working on a threat for Cedric as he

31

walked toward the melon room. The cold air of the vault hit Dave's damp shirt and made him shiver. Watermelons were stacked waist high along the north wall. Nearby John Henry lay on his back, using a narrow, striped melon for a pillow. "Yellow meated." He pointed with his thumb. "Somebody hid it behind the red ones."

"Don't look at me."

John Henry's eyes narrowed. "Somebody didn't want anybody else to find it."

"Aw, come on, Slicker."

"I'm not saying you did it. But I don't know anyone else low enough to."

"Damn you. I ought to kick that thing out from under your head. Besides which if I ratholed a watermelon it wouldn't be none of your business since this is not the John Henry Panky ice plant but the Daddy Warbucks ice plant." Dave glared at him.

John Henry looked away. "Maybe O.P. did it," he said.

Dave dropped to the floor and leaned against the wall. He jerked away as the cold penetrated his shirt, then eased back again.

"You been in to check up?"

Dave shook his head, still angry. Every time John Henry shot off his mouth and had to back off, he acted as if nothing had happened.

John Henry chortled. "You got a big surprise coming."

"You'd best not mess with me," Dave threatened.

"You remember those hayseeds that come up yesterday asking did we need any hands?"

"Yeah."

"Well, Daddy Warbucks hired one." John Henry hugged himself and stamped his feet. "And he's gonna be your helper until O.P. quits."

"I don't need no helper," Dave stormed. He sat up straight, outraged. He was not about to spend his life explaining things to, or waiting for, any hayseed.

"This fella will give you a chance to slow down, have

more time for policy making." John Henry's father was the J. C. Penny assistant manager and took *Fortune* magazine; the slicker repeated everything he read there although he did not know what any of it meant.

Dave blew up. "There ain't no policy on my damn truck, and I'm pretty tired of your *Fortune* magazine crap." John Henry had a gap between his front teeth that was big enough to spit through. Dave threw his ice pick and it buried up to the handle in a watermelon. "Why ain't that hick in the army?"

John Henry giggled. "It ain't the young one. It's the old geezer."

"He's as old as Daddy Warbucks." Dave scooted down on his spine and stared into space. Then he realized that he would have trouble getting by to see Hazel. He felt his eyes getting moist; they were going to have pancakes tomorrow.

"Why don't you strike? The President could take us over like he done Monkey Wards." John Henry retrieved the ice pick and turned the melon's damaged side to the wall. Instead of returning Dave's pick he flopped down and adjusted his green-striped pillow. "You know what Daddy Warbucks did?"

"I don't care."

"A couple of Yankee soldiers come up and bought a watermelon. They cut it right there on the dock, and it was green as a gourd." John Henry caught his sides and rolled over, laughing.

Dave scowled.

"This Yankee asks why ain't it red. Daddy Warbucks says hadn't they heard of yellow-meated watermelons. And they say they have, but probably they haven't. So he says, well, this here is a white-meated one." John Henry was convulsed with laughter. "And they're out there eatin it right now."

Dave's spirits were reviving. "Where?"

John Henry pointed.

Dave peered out the door, then closed it. "Boy, are they gonna be sick."

"And neither one wants to let the other know he doesn't like it."

John Henry was still laughing when Dave left; he spoke to the soldiers as he passed. One had a chunk of white rind on his pocketknife blade. Dave gagged and hurried on to the office. Mr. Blackstone was using the adding machine. He had worn the same pair of trousers every day that summer, although John Henry claimed he was Lawton's eighth richest man. The hayseed, reared back on the hind legs of the cane-bottomed chair, said, "Hidee."

Dave nodded, without warmth. He leaned hard against the table next to the desk and turned his right front pocket inside out. At the sound of the coins Daddy Warbucks glanced up through his heavy glasses. Dave emptied his wallet, and fished the ice coupons from his left rear pocket. He kicked in sixty-seven cents of his own money, from the left front pocket, to pay for the groceries he had taken Hazel.

"Kinda hot, ain't it?" the hayseed asked no one in particular.

When the old man did not answer, Dave said, "A scorcher." He wiped the sweat off his forehead and blotted it on the levis.

Suddenly, Mr. Blackstone whirled about, scooted his swivel chair to the table, and began to stack the coins with a Silas Marner clutch. Something about his attitude toward money — Shy called it "pure dee old greed" — offended Dave; he gazed across the street at Smalley's Grocery. A badly painted sign, red watercolor on brown wrapping paper, was taped inside each window announcing a sale on lard.

Daddy Warbucks coughed, a signal Dave knew. He turned. The old man's back was stiff and his face grave as he studied the careful stacks of coins and currency. "You are three cents short," he announced.

Dave sighed. He shifted so he could get into the left front pocket. He laid down three pennies, and Daddy Warbucks added them to the pile.

"You want to check it?"

"No sir."

"Here it is. Black and white." Mr. Blackstone waved a small piece of paper covered with pinched numbers. It was the same routine every day.

"No sir, sounds right to me."

"You don't have to take my word."

"I can eyeball it and see you are right," Dave lied. From now on he would count his receipts before he came in. A shortage was bad but the old man's behavior was worse when there was an overage. To Mr. Blackstone extra money meant either the employee was sneaking extra ice and spending part of the proceeds or a short-changed customer would be accusing Friendly of sharp practice. No amount of explanation about left-pocket money getting into right-hand pockets would change his mind.

"Okay?"

"Yes sir."

Daddy Warbucks opened the drawer and raked cash and coupons into it. Actually, Dave thought, except for those blue pants, Daddy Warbucks was a fine looking man when he was not snooping or counting money. His gray hair was thick; he always had a tan. Mrs. Blackstone used his Oldsmobile enough to keep him in pretty good condition from bicycling.

Mr. Blackstone beamed. His swivel chair was about halfway between Dave and the hayseed. "David, Elmo here is going to help you until O.P. leaves."

"But . . . ."

"You are a good employee and can make a real iceman out of him."

"Well, I . . . ."

He spun around to face Elmo. "David is one of the better

35

Friendly employees, and I think he can make a real iceman out of you."

The hayseed did not get his mouth open before Mr. Blackstone's back was to him.

"David, Elmo will have to run the route with O.P. for a week or so at the last."

"I just don't want . . .," Dave began, but the owner had already turned away.

"Elmo, you will train with David, but you will work under O.P. awhile before he goes in the army."

Elmo did not attempt a reply.

"But, David, you can't count on Elmo long, because there is no telling when O.P. will go."

By the time Dave said, "Mr. Blackstone, I . . .," the old man was facing Elmo and cautioning him that, "We have no way of predicting O.P.'s induction, so David can't get to depending on you."

"Hell," Dave said, unable to understand why everything had to be repeated. Surely the old man could simply talk to him and let Elmo listen in.

"Yes, David," Daddy Warbucks said, swiveling.

"Nothing."

The employer looked puzzled but said to Elmo, "You must learn fast because O.P. might leave at any time."

Elmo grunted.

"I'm proud of you, Totten," Daddy Warbucks declared, whirling about to face Dave. Over his shoulder he said, "It makes a man proud to have a man like Totten working for him."

Elmo grunted louder since Mr. Blackstone could not see him.

Suddenly Mr. Blackstone was checking an adding machine tape, oblivious to Dave and Elmo. The hayseed came forward with his hand out to be shaken. Dave swallowed hard and said, "Pleased to meetcha, Elmo."

"I got me a boy that's not much older'n you. He's over at North Africa." Elmo reached for his hip pocket; Dave

36

feared he would have to look at a photograph and was relieved when Elmo took out some Brown's Mule chewing tobacco. Elmo offered the plug and Dave declined.

Elmo came just above Dave's shoulders and was almost forty-two years old. He wore heavily starched khaki trousers, a white shirt with curling collar points, a faded purple tie tucked between the second and third buttons of his shirt, and a gray snap-brim hat. His teeth were worn down and tobacco stained. He was probably a good guy, but Dave wished somebody else had drawn him.

Dave left the office still not understanding why he had been unable to refuse to take Elmo. More and more he was learning that good days could come completely apart without warning. He stopped on the dock to ponder his problems. Mr. Smalley's lard sale was not going too well. Scraps of the green watermelon lay where the Yankees had left them. Dave felt sorry for the soldiers, and for Mr. Smalley, and for Elmo. And he was awfully sorry for himself.

A great gob of tobacco juice flew out the office door and splattered on the hot concrete; then Dave was angry.

———————————

John Henry kidded about Elmo until Dave almost beat him up. Dave went down to Theo's for the hamburgers and hot chocolate and he and the slicker ate in the melon vault. There was nothing to do the rest of the day but fill special orders. Dave was so depressed that it did not even help to think about what he and George would do after the war. Dave listened to the slicker recite the contents of *Fortune* magazine and the *Caller-Times*. John Henry exhausted the topic of the B29 and began on how the Democratic party was a club which could choose, if it pleased, to not invite Negroes to join; they could be Republicans. John Henry did read a lot, although he never understood anything. He might well be stupid, but John Henry certainly was not ignorant.

Dave lay on his back, watching his breath cloud and planning how to ditch Elmo when he needed to see Hazel. John Henry sat cross-legged, filing a better point on his ice pick.

"Slicker, you're older than me . . .," Dave began.

"Who ain't?" John Henry said, marveling at his own wit.

Dave remained sullen long enough to show that he required straight answers. "You think old Shirley would go out with me tonight?"

John Henry chunked the pick into the floor and inspected the point. "You bet."

Dave took a deep breath and held it until the cold air made his lungs ache. "I want to love somebody," he said.

John Henry filed off a rough place on the pick. "Old Shirley would like that just fine. Anytime you want it. She thinks you're the greatest thing since the double dip."

"Hell, Slicker," Dave protested, "I don't mean *that*. I've never done *that*." He shut his eyes and wished there was someone he could really talk to. "I mean *love*. Like *in love*, being *in love*."

"Oh," John Henry said in a flat voice. He chunked the pick several times. "I am a lot older than you."

3

"Now, Elmo, you see how we eased her into motion and coasted some before we turned her. We got to do that, because we don't have much by way of brakes, doncha know." Dave glanced at the helper, who nodded. Elmo's ice hooks lay in the lap of his fresh khakis. "Also, if you don't do that, Elmo, you're likely gonna sling the whole damn load out into the street." Dave felt bad about using an old man's given name, but if he said Mister, Elmo might get to thinking that Dave was the helper. "After you finish your turn, speed up. But rush it and you'll lose the whole shebang."

"Uh huh," Elmo said.

Dave resisted the desire to put his foot outside, intending to set a good example. "There's lots to being a iceman." Dave switched on the headlights; he had never gotten to the plant so early before. Probably the slicker was still asleep. He had slept badly; he kept dreaming about Elmo getting there first and driving the truck. Finally Dave woke up and went to work, and sure enough, there was Elmo in the Friendly office chewing Brown's Mule.

It was not until he got to Sadler's Grocery, ordinarily his ninth delivery, that Dave found someone open for business. He slowed to a crawl and stopped behind the bread truck. "Elmo, because we practically ain't got any brakes you can't blare around," he said.

Dave had devised a plan for seeing Hazel; he would work Elmo right down to a nub, make him build up a good appetite, and then leave him somewhere for breakfast. He jumped out and was at the tailgate by the time Elmo's door slammed; he cut a hundred and then a fifty. "Now, see how I followed the scoring saw lines. Don't jab or it will break crooked. Sort of shave it, but go a little deeper every time. Before long you can tell if you're not going to get a straight cut, in which event you make a score line across the top of the block." Dave could not see Elmo's eyes below the hat brim. "Got it?"

"Yep," Elmo answered. "You don't stob."

"I'll take mine to the meat counter. You bring the fifty and wait up front." Dave put the pad on the hundred and tipped it onto his shoulder. Elmo followed, half crouching and holding the hooks with both hands. Dave said, "That goes in the drink box. I'll show you in a minute." He lumbered down the long aisle. The floor, old and soaked with sweeping oil, gave with every step. He passed the candy case and the rack with transparent lids displaying fig newtons, ginger snaps, vanilla wafers, and pink and white marshmallow and coconut cookies. The breadman was trying to revive yesterday's merchandise; the old loaves would go on top of the fresh bread. "How's it going, Taystee?"

The breadman smiled wanly.

Dave turned in behind the meat counter, crossed the butcher's platform, and slid the hundred into a wall box. He made sure no one was watching, then gave the 1939 nude calendar its daily inspection and was surprised at how much women's hair styles had changed. Somebody kept writing dirty things on the calendar, which angered Dave; he wished he had one. Of course, he would have to keep it secret; someone had told him it was against the law to own a photograph of a naked woman.

Dave took a last look, folded his pad, and sauntered toward the bread rack. He wondered whether women posed in the absolute raw, as John Henry said, or if they wore flesh-colored tights, which just had to be the case with someone so pretty and pure. Dave stopped to talk to Taystee. The loaf he was restoring looked as if someone had sat on it. Dave rubbed the toe of his right boot against his left calf, admired the result, and was about to polish the other when he remembered Elmo.

Only the helper's head and shoulders were visible above a Post Toasties display, but he was obviously in a strain. Dave trotted toward the front and found Elmo resting the ice against his legs. His trousers were wet from the knees down. Mr. Sadler and the butcher, who had been in a subdued argument, had stopped to watch Elmo. "Damn, Elmo, you should of put it in." Dave took the hooks and set the fifty on top of the cold drink bottles.

"Hit was gettin heavy," Elmo said.

Dave turned the faucet to drain yesterday's drippings. He showed the helper how to chip so the ice fell between the bottles. "Here again, shave. Hot cokes will blow up if you're rough. Understand?"

"Right," Elmo said. "Don't stob."

Dave introduced Elmo to Mr. Sadler, collected, and trotted back to the truck. He had started the motor and was shifting gears when Elmo caught up. Elmo pressed the wet trouser legs between his palms to encourage the crease.

Dave had to do some real searching to find customers who were open so early. He was afraid he would forget someone later since he was not taking his customers in order. About seven he began making his heaviest stops, setting a fast pace, delivering the cotton compress, the roundhouse, the gins, the highway department, and the new USO building under construction down by the creek. Elmo needed to be caving-in hungry no later than nine thirty.

By the third load, Elmo was showing signs of wear. The crease was out of his trousers. The crown of his hat was crushed from forgetting to duck as he got in the truck. He had ripped his shirt at the compress, and as he wrestled a fifty into the coke box at McGrew's First and Last Chance Gro. and Sta. his tie fell into yesterday's ice drippings. He was breathing hard from running to keep up.

It was almost eight when they reached Jiggs West's Cafe. Out of the corner of his eye Dave watched Elmo give his purple tie the old palm press. Dave followed Elmo inside; the fifty bounced against the helper's leg with every step. The air was sharp with yesterday's onions and today's bacon, and on the nickledeon — the loudest in Lawton by a long shot — Roy Acuff or somebody was singing about a great speckled bird. Jiggs himself leaned, potbellied, red-faced, and satisfied, on the cash register, eating a piece of toast. As the helper reached the end of the counter he boomed, "T-Bone, what in hell do you think you're doing?"

"Hidee," Elmo said, giving Jiggs a pained smile, as he fought the pull of the ice. The Dick Tracy snap was out of his hat, and the brim turned up all around. Dave held the swinging doors as Elmo stumbled toward the icebox.

Dave observed the kitchen with dismay. By all rights half the hicks in Wake County should be dead from eating at Jiggs' place. The cook, a fat man with a three-day growth of beard, had a filthy apron tied around his waist. He wore an undershirt and had a clump of hair on the point of each shoulder. The cook found the ice coupon book beneath a stack of napkins; he handed it to Dave and turned back to the grill, a long-ashed cigarette dangling from his mouth.

Dave tore out a coupon and gave back the book. "Much obliged," he said.

The cook tried to answer around the cigarette, causing the ashes to powder several orders of eggs he was frying. With a quick spatula movement he raked up enough grease to wash away the damage. His eyes met Dave's. He grinned and shrugged.

Dave found Elmo perched on a stool at the counter. Jiggs was serving him a glass of water. One point of Elmo's ice tongs was hooked into his hip pocket.

"Hey, Totten," Jiggs shouted over the din of the crowded

cafe. "Me and T-Bone knowed one another since we was pups."

Elmo agreed.

"By damn," Jiggs roared. "Old T-Bone." He never spoke below a yell, but his customers were so accustomed to the noise that Dave had never seen one look up as Jiggs bellowed greetings to newcomers. "How about some breakfast, Totten? You and old T? Huh?"

Dave said no thanks, that they were running late, which was not true. He wanted to wait for Hazel's pancakes. Besides, he had seen the cook.

Since it was important that Elmo think about food, Dave said, "We can't spare the time this morning, Jiggs, but what would that breakfast have been?" He stood just behind Elmo, so the helper would miss none of the answer.

Jiggs, leaning on the cash register, rolled his eyes back as if he were reading a menu in the top of his head. "Two, three eggs, ham . . . ."

"Ham," Dave echoed right in Elmo's ear. "Or bacon."

"Yeah," Jiggs agreed.

"Or sausage," Dave suggested.

"Yeah, that too," Jiggs answered with enthusiasm. "Maybe little links."

"Golly," Dave exclaimed. He thought he saw Elmo's ear tremble.

Jiggs thundered, "And toast. With jelly." He turned and dropped a fresh slice of bread into the toaster.

"Boy! That sure sounds good! Don't it Elmo?" Dave spaced the statement for best effect.

"And coffee," Jiggs shouted. "And orange juice."

Elmo's hand shook as he sipped the water. He took a chew of the Brown's Mule.

"And potatoes," Dave suggested.

"Oh hell, yes," Jiggs yelled, "a whole raft of them."

Dave whistled.

Elmo was on his feet, the hooks dangling from his hip pocket. He swallowed hard.

43

"Oh Jesus, I forgot somethin," Jiggs roared. "Grits. We got grits this mornin."

"Damnation, Jiggs." Dave put his hand on Elmo's shoulder. He waited for Jiggs' words to sink in, then pitched a nickel on the counter. "Give us some Juicy Fruit gum."

The helper's stomach growled. On the way out Dave handed Elmo a stick of gum and peeled one for himself. Dave stepped on the starter. "That what they call you?" He ground the gears as he shifted. "T-Bone?"

There was a fresh sweat ring above Elmo's faded hat band. He grinned and nodded. "I'll tell you about hit sometime."

"Well, T-Bone, let's deliver some ice." Dave sped up as they started across the graveled market square. The load sounded as if it would knock holes in the truck bed as they hit the bumps. Dave was light-headed — he was hungry all of a sudden — and the truck was out of control. Dave was about to slow down when Elmo rose halfway out of his seat and began yelping like a bronc buster. Hat in hand, he beat on the door and stomped. Dave floorboarded the gas pedal. The truck plunged and bounced and lurched. Dave yelled along with Elmo as the dust billowed up, enveloping the truck and making them cough.

They laughed all the way to the Dyersburg Road. Elmo, his hat on and the snap back in the brim, was leaning against the door, grinning. Dave felt good. He thought about Hazel and then — involuntarily — about Shirley. After last night's movie Shirley said he had the most beautiful teeth she had ever seen.

Dave drove down Pendleton, studying each house so Elmo would not notice his interest in Hazel's place. Her ice card was turned backward, the signal that Ted was gone. He was an infantry training company lieutenant. His chances of being home were slight but Dave always checked. "We better come back later. These people are late sleepers."

Dave was getting a stomachache. He searched for a natural way to bring up the subject of breakfast. The truck was barely creeping as he got back onto Dyersburg. Dave whistled soundlessly.

"How come we're going so slow?"

"Resting the truck." Dave avoided Elmo's eyes.

On the courthouse square were two billboards listing Wake County's servicemen; their names, black and white, were as segregated as the drinking fountains inside.

"My brother's up there."

"So is my boy."

"There's going to be a marble one after the war, for the dead guys." Suddenly Dave was anxious. He said a quick prayer for George's safety.

The speed had fallen so low the truck started to lope. He gave it a little more gas. "You eat a big breakfast this morning, Elmo?"

"Nope."

"What did you have?"

"Buttermilk and cornbread."

"Not much?"

"Not a whole lots."

Although Dave kept his eyes off Elmo he knew the helper was looking at him. The moment was at hand; success would depend on how agonized, and then relieved, he was able to sound. "Elmo," he burst out, "by golly, I think everything is going to work out." Dave smiled sadly yet radiantly.

"How's at?"

"Well, I been so worried about what we did to old Jiggs."

Dave shook his head, held a stern expression for a moment, and put his foot outside.

"What did we do to him?"

"A guy like Jiggs enjoys doing for friends. And his feelings hurt easy. Now, he offered us some breakfast . . . ." Dave's voice trailed off. He wrinkled his forehead and appeared to be undecided again. Then he slammed his

45

fist down on the steering wheel, made a U-turn, and stepped on the gas. "By golly, we're not gonna let Jiggs down. No, by golly, we're not. I will drop you off for that free breakfast, by golly." Dave regretted the overuse of the term "by golly," but he had to keep talking so Elmo would have no chance to object.

"You don't want nothin?"

"No, we can't worry about me, by golly."

Elmo fixed him with a level gaze. "All mornin you been makin it light on me. Now you're gonna deliver more ice while I have breakfast."

"Oh no." Dave was frightened; Elmo was set to out-noble him. "I never eat breakfast. I have to exercise all the time to keep my weight down. Right now I got errands to do for my mother, but we can't let Jiggs down on that," he wanted to lean closer and say the rest directly into Elmo's ear, "free breakfast, the grits and ham and sausage and potatoes and all."

They were at Jiggs' place now, but Elmo made no move to get out of the truck. He was quiet for a long time, then he turned to Dave. "You're a good feller, just like my boy. Why, he would take the world off of my shoulders."

"No. No. You're doing me the favor." Dave reached past and opened Elmo's door. "Really. Honest. You are the only one that can save the feelings of good old Jiggs, by golly. Otherwise he might figure you thought the cooking was dirty."

Elmo wore a fatherly smile.

"You can count the load," Dave pleaded. "I swear I won't deliver one pound of ice." He fought the urge to shove Elmo out.

Finally the helper said, "Go do your chores then."

Not until Elmo was inside the cafe did Dave feel safe. He sped across the square in much the same fashion as before except for the yelling. Dave was ashamed of the lies, but he would make up for them; he would warn Elmo about hanging those hooks from his pocket. If the free

46

point snagged something, the hooks would tear the ass-end out of his pants.

Dave sang "San Antonio Rose" and slapped out the tempo on the steering wheel. He hated hillbilly music but everytime he started to sing it turned out to be something country. At a red light he took Shirley's picture out of his billfold; he did not feel safe having it on him in Hazel's presence. In the photograph Shirley sat on a parked motor scooter wearing loafers and holding a black poodle. Except for skinny legs and a melted-looking nose she was not bad. There was a heavy lipstick imprint on the back of the snapshot; he locked it in the glove compartment so that he was not vulnerable as he went in Hazel's house.

Dave was surprised to find Hazel standing just inside the door. She wore a red pinafore and had a white ribbon in her hair, although Dave had never seen her dressed before noon. She looked like a Lawton High School girl, only prettier. Her stiffness made him uneasy. When he kissed her, she kept her body rigid, crooking one arm around his neck and letting the other dangle. She looked peeved but did not try to move away.

"Yep, I almost didn't make it," Dave said, wondering what was wrong. He looked at the room, hoping for a clue, but all he learned was that she was the only thing around that was cleaned up. On the floor lay a wrinkled yellow apron. Next to the Victrola, on the sofa, was an open movie magazine that had had iced tea spilled on it. "But finally I made it, all right." Dave considered kissing her again, but decided that was her signal to do whatever she had in mind.

"Let's hear hear some music." He tried to sound enthusiastic.

She shrugged. "If you want to."

He knelt and searched through the records. The sound of her lighter behind him meant she was waiting for him to turn around; then she would unload on him. He took his time, and finally she dropped the lighter on the coffee table and stomped off down the hall. "You sure look nice," he called and got an angry silence for his trouble.

Dave put "Body and Soul" on the Victrola and cranked the spring tight. He eased the needle down and went back to the kitchen. Knowing a catastrophe was imminent, he tried to get some spring into his walk. "I say you look pretty this morning."

He found her leaning against the drainboard with a hand on her hip, ready for battle. Then everything went wrong. Dave would not have believed she could talk so loud and fast. First, she knew she had no right to speak since she was only one of his grownup friends and had no claim on him. And even if he were obligated, she would not stoop to mentioning this, because it was impossible to hold any-one against his will. But — and she would rather die than say anything — she happened to be downtown last night, as fate would have it, and was appalled to see him with a skinny-legged, blond-headed girl.

Dave tried to put his hands in his pockets, but they would not fit.

Hazel did not even slow down for breath. She had not been aware that he was in love with someone else or she would have allowed only casual conversation. Of course, Dave thought very little of her and she understood why, but her eyes were open now. She thanked God she had found Dave out before it was too late. She did not care if she ever saw him again; never would be too soon. He had confirmed all her suspicions about men. Because of his treachery, she had wronged her husband, although only in her heart. But she was going to get down on her knees every day and give thanks for her deliverance. And she would be the world's champion wife. Besides, that blond-headed girl had a terrible nose and acted like a ten year old — the only things Dave agreed with in the whole harangue — and he could do better than that. It was all over between him and Hazel, no matter how much he got down on his knees and begged. From now on she was taking ice off of Acme.

Later, Dave tried to remember whether he had said anything and thought not. Before he would have an answer ready she had hit him again. Finally she ran up the hall and returned with the ice card. "Here," she said in a tight voice, holding out the faded cardboard.

Dave pulled himself up to his full height and folded his arms. "Here," she screeched, shoving the card under his nose and then letting it fall to the floor.

"Damn, Hazel," he said.

"Pick it up," she shouted, "and get out of here."

His failure to respond made her more furious. She scooped up the card and began ripping it.

"Well, damn, Hazel."

Her eyes were damp and her chin quivered. She threw the cardboard scraps in his face.

He glanced about, bewildered. "God damn, Hazel," he said and strode past her; in the front room he was pleased to note that the Victrola needle was raking the record label.

He got into the truck and saw Hazel, weeping, pull down the shades. He started too fast, felt the load slide, and hit the brakes, horrified by the prospect of picking up several hundred pounds of broken ice with Hazel watching; the brakes worked well enough to catch the load.

Dave's anger was passing and the hurt was setting in by the time he reached the creek. "I'm through," he told himself. "Finished. Quits with all of them, Shirley, Hazel. Everything in skirts." He picked a fragment of ice card out of his hair.

A train was blocking the Dyersburg Road at the depot. Dave stopped in a line of cars, got out, stretched, and realized how hungry he was. But he had wasted too much time with Hazel to stop for breakfast now. And he could not eat around Elmo after all he had said. Dave was counting on his fingers the hours remaining until lunch when a painful memory intruded. There had been a mixing bowl next to Hazel's stove; anguish swept over him as he realized it held pancake batter.

Elmo, picking his teeth, sauntered out to the truck with the dangling hooks bouncing against his thigh. He scooted down in the seat, and closed his eyes. The purple tie had dried and its tip curled away from his body. "Jiggs sets a purty fair table."

When Elmo asked about the errands, Dave snapped at him. He smiled, to make things all right, but Elmo, acting somewhat wary, said very little the rest of the day.

Hazel's threat to take off Acme bothered Dave although Ace Howard's route was nowhere near her. She might call in a special delivery one day, and Ace might make the delivery. Or being the kind of guy he was, he probably asked every afternoon if anybody had any customers needing banging. Dave was ill; if he lost her he did not want it to be to any Ace Howards.

When he took his last load Dave was in no mood to talk to Cedric, but the plant manager would not leave him alone. He said, "Mr. Sadler claims you delivered his store about midnight, Hotshot, which he appreciates since you're usually late."

Dave assumed he was being praised. He was very hungry even though he had just finished a double handful of snow from under the scoring saw.

Cedric smirked. "What are you up to?"

"You're always watchin me, and you got some real bastard icemen and a building full of machinery that is falling apart." Dave jumped off the dock, and Elmo had to run to catch the truck. He held back the Pendleton deliveries until last; he would have skipped them if he could. Both his head and stomach were hurting.

50

"How come you always know how much to take in?" Elmo asked.

"The window card. It has 25 on one side, 50 on one, 75 on one, and 100 on the bottom. They want whatever's on top."

"Ain't that the beatinest!" Elmo pointed and said, "That house wants a hundred."

"Uh uh, that's Acme's card. They're red and white. We're blue and orange."

They made the Pendleton stops at a gallop. Dave ignored Hazel's house. Since she used fifty pounds a day, and the fight occurred before he took in the ice, she was probably in a bad way. He was sure Hazel was watching as he delivered the neighbors. He threw an arm around Elmo's shoulders and talked loudly as they came out of the house next door. Dave pitched his hooks onto the tarp and gave a hearty laugh.

"You're a odd bird." Elmo seemed confused.

Dave worked up another laugh as he swung into the truck, knowing she was trying to decide whether to let him drive away or attract attention by chasing after him. She had very little sense. All she ever did was lounge around working crossword puzzles, reading movie magazines, guzzling iced tea, and listening to Ma Perkins. Dave felt much better; Hazel was in for a hot, dry afternoon.

————————

Dave was pouring the eighteen hundred thousandth can of brake fluid when John Henry drove up. He did not have to look to know who it was; the sound of the tires, cut hard and scattering gravel, told him. He was depressed. Added to his other troubles was Elmo's aloofness; the helper had been sullen ever since breakfast. Maybe eating made him mean.

John Henry's dust was slow settling; he sat in the truck counting his money. He checked out to the penny every day, which was impossible. To Daddy Warbucks, balancing usually meant that the iceman was taking out more ice than he was putting on the charge sheet and keeping some of the money. But suspicious as he was, Mr. Blackstone could not complain about a man having exactly what he was supposed to, although he did not try to restrain himself when there was a shortage or an overage.

There was little edification in watching John Henry, so Dave went back to the brakes. He had sneaked over to Safeway so Elmo would not know, and consumed three Golden Moon pies and some Hostess cupcakes, which took care of the hunger problem but made him somewhat queasy. He had thought up a number of things he should have said to Hazel; he would use them next time. The trouble was they probably would not fit and he would fare no better than today. Whenever he thought about never seeing Hazel again he became terribly empty.

Dave put the cap on the brake cylinder and dropped the hood. Any other time he would have been aggravating John Henry, but now he could only lean against his fender and gaze into space. Ted evidently let Hazel get away with a lot; he would regret that later.

"Howdy fellers, you need any hands?" John Henry approached with a bumpkin walk, his thumbs stuck into his belt and the hooks dangling from his hip pocket.

"Cut it out, Slicker. He'll see you."

"Who? Who?" The hooks bounced against the slicker's leg. "You need a hand or don't you?"

Dave shoved him away, "Knock it off. Besides you're gonna tear your pants."

"Hit wouldn't kill you to be a mite more neighborly," John Henry brayed, backing out of reach.

"If you don't shut up, I am going to let you have it." Dave brandished the empty brake fluid can. "How come I didn't hear you when you got out just then? I bet you took your door off."

John Henry wilted.

"Sure. Took-off doors don't make slamming noises."

"Nobody can't have any fun with you anymore. You have sure changed for the bad," John Henry complained.

In spite of himself, Dave was sorry. "You check out and let's go eat."

John Henry brightened. "Okay. Let me get my coupons." As he spun about the hooks swung just wide enough to catch the truck bed, and they ripped his left rear pocket from top to bottom.

Dave had examined the message spike several times to see if Hazel had called. He walked to the office with John Henry, looked again, then went down to the melon vault to wait while the slicker checked out.

Dave tried lying down, but he was too nervous about Hazel to keep still. He collected the scattered ice picks, stuck one in the back wall, then threw the rest in an attempt to split the handle of the first one. Robin Hood used to do that with arrows in the Sheriff's contests. But he could not keep his mind off Hazel. He went into the ice vault, scooped up some scoring saw snow, and sat on the dock to eat it. The 1938 Pontiac across in front of the cleaners looked like Grandpa's car. If so, he would be in the saddlemaker's or around the corner at the blacksmith shop; he had friends both places.

As Cedric waited on customers he smirked at Dave from time to time. He did not have the Christian decency to let people alone, which Dave considered pretty bad, especially since Cedric's kid was headed straight for hell. Dave had devised an answer that would really frost Cedric the next time he ordered him to do something.

John Henry came out of the office walking with a sideways slide because of the condition of his pants.

"You ought to pin that up," Dave suggested.

John Henry pulled the torn flap into place and let it fall. "You can't see my shorts."

"No. But the inside of your pocket looks like shorts, so you can just stop and explain that to everybody."

The hostile silence was broken only by John Henry's heels hitting the dock as he swung his legs. Dave pitched the rest of the snow onto the driveway. "Flip you for going after the hamburgers."

John Henry spun a quarter in the air, slapped it against his wrist, and lost. "Aw," he said.

Dave slid off the dock. "I'll go with you, but let's take my Ford. It's easier to get in and out of."

John Henry beamed, displaying the huge gap between his teeth. "Just watch and see if my door is on tomorrow."

"Beat you to the truck," Dave yelled. He sprinted around the corner of the plant, but ten yards from the pickup John Henry passed him, his torn trousers flapping with every step.

Dave parked in the loading zone at the Eatwell Cafe. There was a high curb, with two steps for women and people in tight levis. "Bring your hooks, Slicker, so we'll look like we're making a delivery if Speedy comes along."

Dave ducked under the rolled canvas awning and saw the girl behind the cash register. Her back was to him; her long, black hair came to where the brassiere strap cut its slight outline. Dave stopped and stared, even though the slicker was holding the screen door open and Theo was ready to complain about the flies they were letting in. As Dave entered, the girl turned, looking exactly as he knew she would, and smiled. Dave stepped on John Henry's heel.

"Damn, David, ain't you never seen a girl before?" John Henry said. He spun the tops of the empty counter stools. "My stuff ready?"

"No, it is not." Theo's heavy features were set in a scowl.

To separate himself from the coming argument Dave began studying a menu. He knew he should have waited at the plant. There was trouble every time he went anywhere with John Henry, and it did not take much to provoke Theo.

"How come it ain't ready? We get the same thing every day."

Over the top of the menu Dave watched the girl fill the chewing gum rack. She had dark skin and her eyes were green or blue; Theo was always bringing kinfolks over from Greece. Dave intended to flash the old teeth at the first opportunity. Whatever else Shirley was, she was a good judge of teeth.

Theo bellowed, "I tell you how come. Hot chocolate I cannot sell if you not here. You and this one here make only two people drink hot chocolate in the hundred and ten degree summer of Texas." Theo addressed the bald man at the counter, "What happen if he do not come this day?"

The man shrugged and kept hammering at the catsup bottle.

"What else we gonna drink in a ice vault?" John Henry said, indignantly. "You drink an RC Cola in there and freeze the family jewels."

Theo was kneading his apron. His mouth was set hard and his lower lip protruded. Dave thought sure he was going to mop up the place with John Henry. "What you drink, I do not care. Where you drink it, I also do not care. But hot chocolate I do not make unless you here."

Dave could not get enough of watching the girl.

John Henry said, "The *Fortune* magazine was telling about how courtesy has gone to hell in the business world. They said people like you won't even be able to stay in business after the war."

Dave was so certain Theo was going to swing that he got ready to pull the slicker out of reach.

"I don't have to trade here, you know."

"Shut up," Dave said as he dug his fingers into John Henry's upper arm.

"That hurts." John Henry tried, without success, to pull away.

Dave spoke slowly and softly, "Theo, let us have six hamburgers without onions, please, and a quart of hot chocolate."

The Greek and John Henry glowered at each other for a moment before Theo went into the kitchen. John Henry massaged his damaged arm.

"I ain't coming here with you again, Buddy Boy," Dave told him.

"How come? It ain't my fault that he don't know how to treat customers. I'll show you in *Fortune* magazine."

"You know where you can stick your *Fortune* magazine."

"Well, I wouldn't have a single stop left if I treated customers like he does."

"I just kept you from getting whipped. Now dry up." Dave got to see the cashier up close as he paid the check. Her teeth were very white. She touched his hand when she gave him the change, and Dave thought she said, "Thank you" in a special way.

John Henry was holding the screen door open and acting as if the hot chocolate were burning him through the cardboard container. "Come the hell on," he insisted.

Dave could not recall a time when he wanted so much to clean someone's plow.

4

Hazel's first call, an order for fifty pounds, came while Dave and John Henry were at the Eatwell. Dave had been remembering how the Greek girl, the cashier at Theo's place, sounded when he found Hazel's message. Suddenly it was as if the world were full of gorgeous women who had the hots for him. He and John Henry took the hamburgers and the chocolate to the melon vault. All through lunch Dave imagined how Hazel would get down on her knees when he took the ice to her, if he did take it. They had only a hamburger apiece left when Cedric came in, minus his smirk.

"Hotshot, didn't you see that special order for 814 Pendleton?"

"Not since I started lunch," Dave said.

"She says you missed her."

"I am entitled to eat once a month."

"You skin on out there when you get through."

"Cedric, I already made Pendleton Street. She should of had her card up." Dave was offering only token resistance since he was not sure that he did not want to see Hazel. At the moment he intended to give her up for the Greek girl, but in a little while he would probably be wanting to keep Hazel.

"She called again. Says her baby tore up the card."

Cedric talked around a soggy match stem that he shifted with his tongue. "Says the baby is sick."

Several seconds passed before Cedric's words sunk in. Dave jumped up and yelled, "Baby!"

Startled, John Henry choked and sprayed hot chocolate all over the floor.

Dave was angrily ecstatic. He hated a liar, but Hazel had to be desperately in love with him to lie about something so sacred. "She ain't got no baby. I know that one and all she does is sit out there and smoke cigarettes and drink iced tea. . . . "

Cedric tried to break in, but Dave outshouted him. The slicker, still coughing, mopped the chocolate off his arms with a handkerchief.

Cedric did not give an inch. "You take it out there, baby or no baby."

"You are letting her lie to us about a baby, which is a holy thing to lie about, and then get away with it."

"How come you're so upset?" Cedric leaned against the brown cork wall and began smirking. He was never happier than when he was making life hard for others.

Dave looked at a point about five feet away from Cedric. "There is a war on. We got no business wasting tire rubber and gasoline hauling fifty pounds of ice across town to some damned liar whose only problem is having to drink hot iced tea. If you had a brother flying bombers in England you would not like to waste stuff that maybe he might need." Dave looked to John Henry, hoping for some kind of help. "For all we know she might even have tore up that ice card her own self in some kind of a hissy."

"Hell with her, I say," the slicker announced, coming through at last.

Dave began to be afraid that he sounded too well-informed. "Okay, Ced, I'll take it when I make the USO. But you just go out there, and you will not find one single baby on the premises."

Cedric nodded once and was gone.

"Don't even give you time to eat around here," Dave grumbled.

"That's what I say. And the *Fortune* magazine says employees' work falls off bad if they get upset at lunch." He tried to cough up the rest of the chocolate. Then he went on to tell a number of facts that Dave did not care to know, but Dave was tolerant.

Dave felt great. Hazel was scared to death she would never get to see him again. As Dave lifted the hamburger he tensed and admired his forearm muscles. He would go straight out there so she could beg his pardon for getting jealous.

"You better make that delivery," John Henry warned. Dave shrugged. He flipped his ice pick, and it buried to the hilt in a watermelon. John Henry retrieved it. Dave tried to sound casual. "You notice the girl at the Eatwell?"

"Boy, that Theo burns me up."

"You ever seen her before?"

"Someday I'm going to reach across that counter, and . . . ." John Henry laid down his hamburger and slammed a fist into his palm, enraptured by prospects of the violence he would do. He retrieved the hamburger and was about to take a bite when he snapped his head toward Dave. "Hey, I seen the way you was lookin at her. Don't think you got away with nothin."

"Has she been in town long?"

"Old Theo better watch his step is all I got to say, unless he wants to be a Greek grease spot."

Elmo came in with his syrup bucket and hunkered down for awhile, but his conversation got in the way of Dave's thinking about Hazel and the Greek girl, so Dave told him to go home.

"Okay then, if you don't need me." Elmo shifted the bucket from one hand to the other.

"Yeah," Dave said, "you did good today."

"Sure, go on," John Henry added.

Dave glared. "Just shut up. He's not your helper."

After he finished lunch John Henry started shadow boxing. "I'm freezin," he said.

"Your blood is thin."

John Henry's long skinny arms and legs made him look like a huge grasshopper dancing. "You want a date with old Shirley tonight?" Patsy kept the pressure on John Henry to have Shirley dated.

"Please!" Dave said, making a face. "I'm still eating."

John Henry stopped in mid-jab. His jaw went slack. "That was a stinking thing to say."

"Yeah, I guess it was."

The admission deflated John Henry, who was getting ready to shame Dave into taking Shirley out. All he could manage was a weak, "How about tonight?"

"I didn't sleep good, and I had to get up right after the midnight news to beat that farmer down here."

John Henry sighed, "That means Shirley will go with us then. And she talks all the time. I can't get Patsy off by herself except when somebody takes over Shirley."

Dave said with mock sincerity, "Much as I'd like to, Slicker, I just can't."

John Henry flared up. "When that Greek girl won't have nothing to do with you, don't pester me about old Shirley. Because somebody that has some brains will have her all sacked up by then." He waited around for awhile, and when it appeared that Dave would not change his mind, John Henry stalked out with the torn trousers flapping.

———————————

The house was quiet. Mother had gone shopping and Ellis was at the tree house. Dave took one of the blue cushions out of the sofa and threw it down on the rug. He did a pushup and lowered himself to the floor. From there he could see the sepia photograph of George on the mantel. Dave wished he had George's class. George always had a handkerchief sticking out of his breast pocket when he dressed up, and he used after shave lotion, which Dave could never remember on those infrequent occasions when he had to shave. Even George's jobs had more tone; he caddied at the country club and clerked at the Haberdashery Shoppe. Dave had spent his life delivering things, but he did have good taste in women. Hazel was awful good-looking. And George would have to admit the Greek girl was a knockout, although she was not George's type. That is, she was nothing like Mary Mooney, who would be George's wife one day.

Dave had been asleep for perhaps an hour when he heard the racket in the kitchen. He was dreaming about the Greek girl and did not want to wake up. He thought for awhile that Ellis and his crew would get quiet or go outside. Finally he realized he could not recapture the dream; he put the cushion back in the sofa and walked toward the noise. The T-shirt was stuck to his chest, and he wiped sweat off his forehead. As he opened the kitchen door everything became very quiet. Four dirty faces stared at him.

"Where is Mother?"

"I dunno," Ellis said, "out buying things, I guess."

Dinty came over to Dave to be petted.

"What's all the fuss?"

Ellis said, "Aw nuthin. We was dividin up the peanut butter, and T. A. got too much." The only time Ellis looked good was in the presence of his friends. They were even dirtier than he was. Their hair was wilder, they were harder on their clothes, and today they were even sweatier than Ellis. Each of his friends had a bowl into which Ellis was spooning peanut butter. They were going to eat it straight. Dave's mouth went dry.

"You sure are going to be thirsty, T. A.," Dave said.

The whole crowd disputed him.

Dave said, "Go ahead, but you got to eat it all, every one of you."

T. A. cheered. "Oh boy," Reedy exclaimed. "Thanks, Mr.

61

Totten," Otho said; he had a heavy dirt necklace above his Adam's apple.

"Don't call me mister, Otho. I'm just sixteen."

The friends crowded in as Ellis handed them spoons and doled out the balance of the quart of peanut butter. Dave looked at the thermometer that hung beneath the eaves; it read a hundred and two.

"And you, Ellis, wash those dishes afterwards. And don't just run water. You got to rub peanut butter to get it off."

Ellis had taken a big bite and could not answer.

"You hear me? If mother finds a mess you got bad trouble."

Ellis squared his shoulders and tried to chew far enough through the peanut butter to give a smart answer.

Watching them made Dave thirsty. He got his copy of *See Here, Private Hargrove*, ran some water into the bathtub, and shed his work clothes. He looked funny in the raw now. His legs, deep brown from years of football practice, were matched by his neck and face and his arms below sleeve level. He needed to go to the pool and even out his color. He put the book and a towel on the floor and climbed into the tub. With his left foot he turned on the hot water again and settled back to see what Hargrove did next.

Private Hargrove and his friends were not shooting at Japs or Germans, but they were where the army put them. That probably made them feel pretty good, Dave decided. Unless a man was in service or working at the bomber plant he could do little to win the war except maybe worry and try not to make things hard on others. Dave was too young for the army or a defense job, but he never stopped feeling guilty about George and the others fighting while he lived a normal life. From time to time the back screen slammed. Once Ellis' bunch came down the hall and Dave shouted, "You idiots play outside."

Ellis yelled that it was his house, too, and took his friends upstairs. Then there was running on the stairs and down

62

the hall. Dave shouted threats as the screen door slammed rapidly three times. He stayed in the tub until he was drowsy and got the edge of the book wet. He dried, sprinted up the stairs with a towel around his waist, and fell across the bed.

Hazel had probably chewed her nails all afternoon, waiting for him and that fifty. When she realized he was not coming she would cry, then get all sharped up and give Ted the big hello. He would have to take her out, because she would refuse to sit around the house all dressed up. Everywhere they went she would be trying to catch him with old Shirley. And Ted never would figure out what had happened. Dave closed his eyes and was sad about Hazel and the way it could have been if he were older.

From the vacant lot came the sound of crossed sticks and tin cans being hit, which meant Ellis had a shinney game going. Before long there would be a falling out and somebody would leave bawling.

Dave forced his mind away from Ellis. He tried to remember how the Greek girl looked but could not. He turned on the radio. Levi Hackley was starting his afternoon line of bull. Levi was always taking screen tests, but nothing ever came of them; he had lots of ducktailed hair and drove an old white convertible and talked like an Englishman. But Levi did play better music than the other record programs, which made it almost worth enduring Levi's "yes, yes" trademark and listening to the theme song — written and recorded by Levi — at least once each hour.

"And now," Levi said, "we're going to play 'Miss You' for all the gang down at Billie's and over at the Dutch Inn."

Dave tried to recall the Greek girl's face, but she kept turning into Hazel.

" 'Miss You'," Levi said and gave some information about Kay Kyser that everyone knew. "And from Dyersburg a request for Marie and Dorothy and Paul and Marjorie and Billie Ann and Marsha and Jean Kay, from one who cares."

Later, Dave put on a white shirt and gray trousers and went downstairs. Surprisingly enough, Ellis had washed the bowls clean and left them, bottoms up, to dry. Dave thought it was a sign of growth, but then he noticed water on the floor. The first spot was football-sized, the others smaller; they led out the back door.

Dinty was asleep next to his house. Beside his water pan was a huge mound of peanut butter on a newspaper. Dave stalked out to the tree house. The shinney players had left their sticks at the entrance. Dave bent and stuck his head inside where the temperature was at least two hundred degrees. "Ellis," he snapped, "did Dinty eat any of that peanut butter?"

"I dunno. Some, maybe." The little brother sat in the dark with a glass of ice water he had just dipped from the pressure cooker. In addition to T. A., Reedy, and Otho, there were two others Dave did not know. Each held a glass and tried to be inconspicuous.

"Well, here is some advice for you. Number one is that Mother will be here soon. Number two, she is going to be upset over that spilled water. Number three, she will throw a hissy if you didn't refill the ice trays. Number four is that she will bust a gut if she finds that cooker and those glasses out here. Number five — and you better pay special attention to this — I will whip your tail if you get Dinty sick on peanut butter."

"You talked ugly about our mother," Ellis charged. "You said gut."

Dave moved forward a step, and all the occupants, except Ellis, recoiled. "I mean what I say."

"You know so much." Ellis pitched the rest of his water toward Dave. It was not far enough to wet Dave but impressed the little brother's friends.

Dave seethed. He should straighten out Ellis right then, but he would ruin his clothes in the tree house; Ellis knew when he could get away with smarting off. Dad was right, the lot ought to be plowed and planted for a Victory garden.

———————————————

Dave finished off a malt and hamburger and ordered a second round while he summoned the nerve to talk to the Greek girl. He endured thirty minutes of Theo's tirade against John Henry in hopes she would decide he was a special friend of the management.

The Eatwell was full of soldiers. Dave did not like the way they lingered at the cash register; probably every one asked the Greek girl for a date. The only time she looked at Dave was when he came in. He showed his teeth then, but she seemed not to recognize him. Dave watched her make change and answer the telephone. Each time he almost had enough nerve she would laugh or say something to a soldier, and his resolve would go. Then, of all the damned people in the world, Ace Howard came in and bought a comb. When she laughed at something Ace said, Dave almost decided she was too depraved to be worth the bother. He came close to just saying to hell with all of them: Hazel, Shirley, and the Greek girl. But finally Dave got in line at the register. He had rehearsed a speech, but as he handed her the dollar bill everyone in the line pushed up closer to see what he was going to say; half the United States Army was going to hear him get turned down.

"Was everything all right?" She still acted as if she had never seen him before.

"Uh huh. Yes. Fine. Very all right." Dave grabbed his change and bolted for the door. He did not regain control until he reached the Friendly plant; by then he had stopped trying to decide when "very all right" would be a proper answer. There was nobody in the office. He sat in Daddy Warbucks' swivel chair beneath the naked light bulb and peered into the dusk. It was a safe kind of a place. The

65

walls were varnished pine and the floor was concrete. The heavy machinery sent tremors through the building.

Dave picked up part of a *Star-Telegram* someone had been reading. A headline, "Workers Run Sex Lottery," caught his attention. Two Seattle bomber plant lady employees had sold tickets for a lottery in which they were the prizes. Dave did not believe any woman would do such a thing, but he liked stories like that.

Suddenly Dave remembered the phone spike. He jumped up and flipped through the messages. Five were Hazel calls. One mentioned the baby tearing up the ice card. Two talked about the baby being sick. One said, "Totten, call customer at 814 Pendleton. Number is 352." The last slandered Dave terribly, claiming he put a fifty on top of a pound of soft butter and kicked over her ice pan and did not clean it up. She was switching to Acme unless Dave was there by ten o'clock tomorrow. The most galling thing was her failure to use his name; she called him the iceboy.

Nothing ever worked out with women. Dave threw the notes into the wastebasket. Then, on the chance that Daddy Warbucks might find them, he burned them in the ashtray. One fell out and scorched the desk. He ought to swear off women, so he could use all his time constructively, like planning the taxi company.

Just as Dave started to call the Greek girl Cedric came through the office in a tie and a suit with a belt in the back, said, "Hello Hotshot," and disappeared into the machinery room.

Dave put down the receiver and covered the burned place with the newspaper. Knowing Cedric would not be gone long, he busied himself studying the telephone directory. Cedric came back through and went into the ice vault.

Dave gave central the Eatwell number and waited, hoping to finish the conversation before Cedric returned. The telephone rang several times. Maybe nobody would answer. Maybe he could write off the Greek girl without having to talk to her. Relief swept over Dave. But then the receiver was lifted. Her voice was softer than he remembered.

"This is David Totten. I am . . . ."

"I know who you are."

"You do!" he exclaimed, so excited he almost added that he knew who he was, too.

"Yes."

"Well, I am David Totten, like I say, and . . . ."

"Just a minute, please." She went off the line. Dave could hear the cash register and the murmur of conversation. Some damned soldier was wasting her time. Suddenly he was fed up with guys trying to put the make on her and furious with her for leading them on.

"I'm back," the soft voice said.

"Well, I . . . ."

"No, it's for me," she called to someone in the cafe. Then to Dave, "I'm sorry."

"Well, I was wondering what your name was, and . . . ."

"Just a sec." She dropped the receiver again.

Dave swung his feet up onto the desk, boiling. She had no business working down there with all those soldiers. If he were her father, Theo would be looking for a new cashier. She laughed at something that Dave did not hear and he was about to hang up when she said, "Sue. Sue Wales."

Her voice killed the anger and made him fear that he might never hear it again. He hurried so he could get an answer before another interruption, "I wanted to know could I walk you home."

"I'll be right back," she said, and was gone.

Dave covered the mouthpiece and used the filthiest language he knew. Cedric heard him as he came in. He shook his head and smirked. He took some change to a customer in an old Dodge that gave off lots of smoke, then leaned against the wall right above Dave, who tried to ignore him. Cedric looked awful when he was dressed up. "What you got cooking, Hotshot?"

"Oh," Dave lied, "I'm just calling my mother."

"Good!" Cedric dragged a chair over close to Dave and sat down. "Mind if I say hello? Did I ever tell you we went to high school together, me and Vivian?"

"Yes, damn you Cedric, you have told me eight million times."

Cedric did not move nor did he drop that phoney friendly expression of his. "Did you know she was a cheerleader? Or was it a drum majorette? Or a Rainbow girl?"

Dave leaned as far away as he could, hoping to scare Cedric by the way his mouth was set so hard and his forehead was so deeply wrinkled. Dave snarled, "This is a private conversation."

"No, David, I was wrong about that. I'm sorry. She was sweetheart of the class. That's what she was. I haven't talked to her in years."

When the Greek girl came on the line again, Dave turned his back to Cedric. She said, "I guess it would be all right. I have to tell Daddy not to come for me."

Cedric poked him in the ribs. "Ask her whether she was a cheerleader."

Dave clapped his hand over the mouthpiece and threatened the plant manager. "What time would that be?" Dave said in a low voice, glaring at Cedric, who gave no sign of going away.

"I don't understand," she said. "You mean what time do I get off?"

"Uh huh."

Cedric got up and spread his arms as if he were on stage. "We had a class song I could sing for you, Hotshot." Dave kicked at him but as he missed his elbow knocked the *Star-Telegram* off the scorched place on the desk.

"Is somebody there?" the Greek girl asked.

"Yeah." Dave wished he knew her well enough to tell the truth, that he had with him a real, true-life, flesh and blood, genuine, cigarette-smoking, matchstick-chewing, son-of-a-bitch.

"I'm off at ten."

"Cheerleader. Ask her," Cedric repeated. He saw the burned desk top. "Somebody has been playing in the fire and I am going to have to make out a report to our employer. Do you know anything about it?"

"I'll be there." Dave kicked again and almost fell out of the swivel chair. He put the earpiece down and tried to hold onto the sound of her voice. He moved the *Star-Telegram* back over the burn. "Cedric, you are damn lucky that I have a good disposition."

When he had a tie on, Cedric's neck looked like a turkey's. He said, "I waited all this time and you didn't let me speak to Vivian.

Dave decided not to stoop to answering him.

"And I note you got so excited reading about those tainted women in Seattle that you scorched the old gentleman's desk."

Dave wished he had caught Cedric with one of those kicks; he was too angry to express his full bitterness. "Christ Cedric, I feel sorry for Warren and your other kids."

Cedric tried to look sympathetic. "Well Hotshot, I just hope my children are as thoughtful about calling their mother as you are about calling yours."

Dave took his time getting home. There was a full moon and a breeze that moved the branches and leaves so slightly he was not sure there was really any motion. He walked several blocks out of his way; everything seemed strange and unreal. Finally he was at home. Light shone from the living room windows. Dave stopped on the sidewalk and watched the family; it was still too hot to have the windows down or the blinds drawn. Mother was on the sofa looking down and talking to Ellis, although Dave could not see him. Dad puffed on his pipe and read a magazine. Sometimes his glasses reflected the light and he seemed to have no eyes at all. The big walnut radio in the corner was playing. It was strange to be standing outside; being dead was probably something like that. What they felt for one another should tell them he was there. A long time ago in Sunday School Dave saw a painting of Christ standing outside a house, and he had thought of Dad's little brother, Georgie, who was the only dead person Dave knew anything about. Dave used to wonder if Georgie — George was named for him — ever watched the family. Sometimes he would want to go outside and find Georgie and bring him in. Dave shivered in the warm summer night, said a prayer for George and Georgie, and went in.

"Have you had your supper?"

"Yes ma'am." He sat on the sofa and put his arm around her.

"How come you're in so early?" Dad said, meaning he should have been home all evening.

"I have to leave in a little while," Dave said.

Dad clamped down on the pipestem. He dropped the magazine and snatched up the newspaper from the floor.

"We're glad you're here." Mother touched his cheek.

Ellis was sprawled before the radio listening to Mr. District Attorney, worried about the crooks making off with Miss Miller to get the D.A. to do or not to do something. Somebody stole Miss Miller every week, but Harrington and the D.A. were always surprised.

Dinty was asleep at Dad's feet, the tip of his pink tongue showing. Dad did not take his eyes off the paper as he asked, "Where you going?"

Dave answered even though he preferred to not discuss his business before Ellis. "This girl, Sue Wales. I'm going to walk her home."

"Home from where?" Lately Dad was always angry; his hands shook and rattled the paper.

"She works at the Eatwell. I think she runs it when Theo isn't there." Dave was reluctant to call the Greek by his first name; Dad insisted that he show respect for old people. But Dave could not pronounce Theo's last name and doubted if Dad could either.

"Is she a nice girl?" Mother was small and trim. She liked crossword puzzles and the daily serial in the *Caller-Times*. The light made her seem grayer than she really was.

"Yes, ma'am. I think she's Greek."

"Homer's a Greek," Ellis said.

Dave was irritated at first because the name seemed to fit one of Ellis' friends, but then Dave remembered the *Iliad* and *Odyssey* book he gave Ellis last Christmas and was pleased that it had made such an impression. Dave said, "Yeah, he sure was."

Dad threw the paper down. "She couldn't be much if her parents let her run around at all hours with some worthless kid."

Mother cleared her throat and gave Dad a hard look. She had the *Caller-Times* folded to the current serial, "Murder in Hollywood." She said to Ellis, "No sleeping down there. You have a bath to take."

"I'm not asleep," Ellis said. "I listen with my eyes shut."

She stirred the air with the Garrett Snuff fan. "You can hear to the end of the program."

"I should think," Dad said, struggling with his temper, "that you could spend more time at home."

"I am here. A lot of the time."

"I won't abide that, David. You will not talk back to me. You eat and sleep here. Otherwise, you're Lord knows where." Dad went to the mantel and scraped the bowl of the pipe into an ashtray. He and George used to argue a lot; George would get as angry and loud as Dad, but

71

Dave could never bring himself to do that. He simply pulled into himself.

The noise woke Dinty. He waddled over and collapsed in front of the sofa. Mother patted his head. "Poor old fella. He's not been feeling good. When I came in this afternoon, Malvin, he had thrown up all over the back steps."

Remembering the peanut butter, Dave looked at his little brother, who had been all eyes from the time Dad raised his voice but was now pretending to be asleep. Dave waited for him to open an eye.

"You know, he isn't really that old, Malvin, to be getting sick and all. But maybe dogs age like people. Maybe some get old faster than others."

"Could be."

If Ellis was peeping he was doing a good job of it, but he would forget himself. Dave said, "I drove Grandpa home yesterday."

"That so?" Dad was getting over his mad. "Vivian, see if they'll come for dinner Sunday."

Mother was relieved. "That would be nice. Maybe your little girl could come too, David."

Dave nodded. He picked up the fan; it had a bird dog painting on one side and a Garrett's Snuff ad on the other. Ellis' eyes remained closed, but he was jiggling his foot as the crooks were about to do in Miss Miller. Dave twirled the wooden handle between his palms. The program ended with Harrington gee whizzing about the D. A.'s shrewdness in getting Miss Miller back and solving the crime. Mother got Ellis up and he pretended to be walking in his sleep. Only when he was safely into the hall did he open his eyes. He made a face at David and disappeared into the bathroom with Mother.

Dad filled and tamped his pipe and dropped into the old green chair. "Be with your grandparents while you can."

"I will."

"Your mother won't let on about it, but she worries

72

about George constantly. You have to show her more attention." He studied the pipe. "George is so far away. So many things could happen to him, and it would take so long for us to hear that she always thinks he might already be hurt and we just don't know." He raised his glasses and rubbed the places where they pinched his nose.

"Yes sir." Dave was afraid he was going to cry. He felt guilty, as if somehow he had put George in danger. When he thought about it, most of his feelings about George were selfish. He wanted to spend time with George, but more than anything Dave wanted George to know that he was grown up. If George did not come back, if he died, he would remember Dave as a child — would see him as he saw Ellis — through all eternity. Dave swallowed hard and stared at the print of the bowed Indian at the end of the trail that had hung in the living room since first he could remember. Dave wished nothing would ever change.

5

Dave brushed his teeth twice, ate half a box of Sen-Sen, which he detested, and got to the Eatwell ten minutes early. He took a corner table after making sure the Greek girl saw him. He sat with his back to the kitchen, hoping Theo would not notice. The cafe was full of soldiers who acted as if they had no place to go. Dave thought they blew a bugle at Camp Norris and everybody had to be in the sack, but it was almost ten and nobody was in a hurry.

Porky Witt, Carl Long, and Jim Ball came in and sat down at his table, although Dave had tried to appear so engrossed in reading the menu that they would leave him alone. Porky popped him on the upper arm with an extended knuckle, raising a frog.

"That's junior high stuff, Pork."

Porky sniffed. "Sen-Sen," he announced and everyone laughed.

Dave glanced at the clock; he certainly did not want to introduce Porky and the others to Sue, and he did not want her to think he had decided to be with them instead of taking her home. Dave yawned and announced, "I got to get to bed."

"Aw come on." Porky grabbed his arm.

Dave's first reaction was to slug him, but he jerked

loose, forced another yawn, and said, "Six o'clock comes early."

"You ain't goin home carrying all that Sen-Sen," Long stated.

Dave picked up the check, stretched, and got in line. He had ordered a glass of iced tea so he would feel right about sitting at a table but he had not touched it for fear of ruining the effect of the Sen-Sen. Dave tried to catch the Greek girl's eye, without success. She was developing a bad habit of ignoring him. Maybe she had changed her mind about going with him. Or her folks had insisted on coming for her. Or she was mistaken about who he was when he called; maybe she had thought he was Ace Howard.

Dave resented her friendliness toward the customers. Somebody like Ace Howard would think she was promising him something. He put down the check. The clock, through its grease-stained glass front, showed it was ten, right on the money.

"Everything all right?" she asked in the same tone and with the same smile she used with all the others.

"Fine." Then, dropping his voice, he added, "I'll wait at the corner."

She gave him a cashier's smile and nodded, which could have meant anything.

Dave went outside. He had intended to flash the old teeth, but he was too badly hacked. It was necessary that he keep in mind that he had to get to know her before he could straighten her out. He stood at the curb and looked at the sky. Everything was all right. She knew who he was and was just maintaining appearances.

Above Theo's place the sign kept blinking "Eat. Eat. Eat." Neon signs marked most of the important places along the Dyersburg Road. Across the street was the Acton Inn; John Henry called it the "Action Hotel" and said it was a cat house. Two naked light bulbs hung over the Acton's entrance, attracting moths. Dave watched a beat-up taxi stop and discharge a load of drunken soldiers. The driver collected the fares and then tried, unsuccessfully, to start the motor; the soldiers, with much shouting, pushed until the engine turned over.

The Eatwell was emptying. A corporal leaned on the cigar counter talking to the Greek girl so other customers had to go around him to pay their checks. Disappointment, fear, anger, and jealousy welled up in Dave. Probably she had promised the corporal he could walk her home, too. Girls never kept their word, besides which Dave had read that Greeks were awfully hot natured; some were nymphos, even. He walked down to the corner so he would not have to face the corporal and the Greek girl when they came out.

It seemed the whole town knew that David Totten was waiting at the intersection of Dyersburg and Foxworthy to get stood up. He hoped none of his friends would see it. He moved out of the flow of traffic, crossing the street and going up the post office steps. It was 10:05 by the clock inside. Dave took his time sauntering back to the corner, then he let the traffic signals change half a dozen times, promising that if she did not come out in three minutes he would dismiss her from his life forever.

The Eatwell's door opened and the corporal came out. He talked to someone inside for a moment. Dave got ready to leave if the Greek girl followed the soldier. Then the corporal let the screen door slam and came toward Dave. He spoke and Dave returned the greeting, feeling much better; actually the soldier was just a long way from home. Dave watched him into the next block, and when he turned back the Greek girl was standing on the sidewalk looking about. Dave barged into the street against the light and sprinted across to her. "I was getting to worry," he said.

"About me?"

"Yes. Uh huh."

She was all color; her black hair framed a brown face,

deep red lips, and white, white teeth. Dave held her purse and tried to help her into the sweater. "Which way?"

She pointed south. Dave caught her elbow as they stepped off the curb and waited for the light. Weakly Washington drove by in his old pickup. Half a dozen of his kids rode in the back; one dragged a toy tractor at the end of a piece of binder twine.

"Weakly was a customer on my *Star-Telegram* route. I guess he is startin to celebrate Juneteenth."

"What?"

"Emancipation Day. It's tomorrow."

"Oh." She was not interested, which was unfortunate, since Juneteenth then constituted a hundred per cent of his ready conversation. He released her elbow when they reached the other curb; he wanted to hold her hand but was afraid to try.

Sue talked about her father, who was a sergeant stationed at Camp Norris, and her mother, who hated Texas summers, and the little girl next door, who said funny things. Dave caught little of it. His main concern was with how to slow her down so they did not reach her home too soon and how, safely, to hold her hand. She fell silent. It was his time to talk, but he could think of nothing but holding her hand. He was frantic. "Uh, see that house over there?" Dave pointed. "I used to know a guy lived there. Turner was his name. He's in the navy. Old Steve Turner."

It was a bad start. She seemed as puzzled as when he mentioned Juneteenth, but she courteously attended to the former home of Steve Turner of the United States Navy. Having nothing else to contribute he said, wistfully, "Old Steve Turner."

"I knew a boy named Turner back home." She studied the house. "In Oregon."

Dave was grateful for her good manners. "I don't know whether old Steve had any relatives in Oregon or not."

"The boy I knew was Arthur Turner."

Dave sighed. "Steve may have had a cousin or two

77

named Arthur, all right, but I never did know about them."

"It's a small world."

Dave was miserable. He stared at the cracks in the sidewalk. "Actually, I never did know old Steve. He was lots older than me. But I heard my brother, George, talk about him."

"Oh," she said.

He fell silent. They were almost past the house now. "Anyhow, that's where he lived. I think."

She cast one last long appreciative look at the house.

Dave swallowed hard. He felt like crying, or saying something dirty, or throwing himself in front of a truck. The back of her hand kept brushing his, but there was no inconspicuous way to grab it. Things had not been so difficult with Hazel or Shirley. He had never been hard up for something to say to them. "I used to have a paper route down here, too." They were walking about a yard apart by then. "Nobody ever throwed papers as many different places as me."

The Greek girl did not respond; her silence terrified Dave. The whole thing was a bust. Dad was right. He ought to stay home every night, work crossword puzzles with Mother, read "Murder in Hollywood," make a decent human being out of Ellis, and study up on the war so he would be ready when his time came.

Dave increased the pace. He would deliver the Greek girl and wash his hands of all women and be pure and wise and strong. He felt her watching him for a long time before he risked looking. She was grinning, which was the most aggravating thing she could do. He would introduce her to Porky, who thought it was great fun for him and his date to tickle one another. "What?" he demanded.

"Mildred Fox told me all about you," she stated.

"She did?"

The Greek girl nodded.

Dave stepped in front of her. "The Orphan Annie decoder pin? Us washing her hair in gasoline? Her getting hit in the mouth with the mud ball?"

Sue started first; then he was laughing hard. The street lamp over the intersection swung with the wind. "And playing pop the whip?" Dave was laughing too hard to continue. "She got flung against the schoolhouse and busted her arm?"

He backed off and staggered around this way and that. Her shoulders shook and she tilted her head back from time to time. The town was filled with their laughter, and when Dave put his arms around her there were tears down her cheeks.

She became aware of the world before he did. She glanced about, and tried to quiet him. For awhile, they worked at stopping laughing and getting so they could look at each other without starting again. He caught her at the waist and lifted her to arms' length overhead. He held her there until his arms began to tremble. Then he let her down slowly, and kissed her as the dancing street lamp brought them from darkness to light and back again.

They sat on Sue's front porch until almost one o'clock when her father began slamming doors all over the house, signaling for her to come in. They pretended not to notice until they heard footsteps heading for them.

"He's going to turn on the porch light, and I'll just die if he does," Sue said. She jumped up, pecked Dave, and went inside.

Dave hurried across the yard with the same apprehensiveness he had known as a halfback about to be tackled from the blind side. He reached the safety of Foxworthy Street without looking back. By the time he got downtown he was very hungry. Dave went in the back door of the

Little Brownie Bakery; the sudden brightness of the lights made him blink.

"Hey, Lud," Dave yelled to one of the sweating, white-clad men, "I'm getting some doughnuts." The bakers ignored him as he passed through the huge open space in the back of the building and entered the darkened sales-room. He knelt behind the glass case; finding no sacks, he put the doughnuts on a piece of waxed paper and went back into the bakery.

"Hey, Lud, here's two bits." Dave put a quarter on the table with the telephone. No one paid any attention to him.

Dave drifted homeward, licking his fingers between doughnuts, wishing the night would not end, and saying her name again and again. Once he read a poem about Jenny kissing somebody. "Sue Wales kissed me," he said, but could not recall enough of the poem to make it work. The doughnuts ran out as Dave reached home; he pitched the wax paper, sticky with sugar glazing, into the doctor's front yard.

Dave tiptoed into the house and undressed in the dark. He went to the window and studied Sue's earrings by the moonlight, then dropped them into the desk drawer. But the situation disturbed him — it was like putting Sue and Shirley in touch — so he removed Shirley's earrings; he would keep them in the glove compartment of the truck until he decided what to do.

Dave sat on the side of the bed trying to recall all that had happened. He could not reproduce Sue's face in his memory nor could he remember exactly how she talked. All he knew for certain was that he had rather be with her than with anyone else. No matter how crazy Hazel and Shirley were about him, it looked as if they both had been shot out of the tub.

Dave dreamed of Sue all night, and Mother had to call him only once next morning. He was in good spirits, so when Elmo arrived carrying his Br'er Rabbit lunch bucket, Dave welcomed the helper as if he had not seen him in weeks.

Elmo returned a cautious greeting. His hat still had the Dick Tracy snap, and the tip of the purple tie stuck out, but there was something different about him.

"You want to pull the truck around?" Dave asked, feeling a vague good will toward everyone.

The helper grinned. He took his lunch inside while Dave worked the key out of the pocket of the tight levis.

"Have at her." Dave pitched the key, and Elmo, coming out of the office, and not able to see very well, missed it.

Dave was helping Shy load out when Elmo eased the truck· around the corner. Dave noted, with disgust, that the helper's foot was on the running board. "Wait there till we finish loading Shy," he shouted. "And get all your damn feet inside."

Elmo nodded. He stepped on the brake, but the orange Ford, pointed toward Shy's truck, did not slow.

"Pump em. Pump em," Dave yelled.

Elmo's brake leg went like a piston and he was still stomping the pedal when the truck hit Shy's Plymouth hard enough to throw Elmo into the windshield and pitch his hat out onto the concrete apron.

Dave had not been able to move since Elmo began closing on Shy's truck. Elmo scrambled out, retrieved his hat, and got back behind the steering wheel.

Shy's round face was flushed. He said, "Christ, Totten, teach the silly bastard how to herd that thing."

"Aw dry up," Dave snapped, "you damned Arkansas hillbilly." The fact that the helper had been showing off, trying to act like an iceman, was none of Shy's business. Dave could step on his own helper. He intended to tear up Elmo until he saw how badly shaken he was, so he just said, "Don't let it get you down none."

After Shy left, Dave had Elmo back the truck up to the dock. Elmo was reluctant to drive, but Dave had seen a movie that showed the best cure for a scared paratrooper to be making another jump right quick.

Dave's high spirits soon returned. The Greek girl made everything different. He was extra nice to Elmo, and he even felt sorry about Hazel spending all that time without iced tea yesterday. It was not until they reached the compress that Dave realized what was different about the helper. "By golly, you got new levis," he exclaimed.

Elmo blushed.

"They gonna fade all over your legs, but you're gonna like them." Dave was pleased; until then he had been the only iceman in Lawton who wore T-shirts and levis. "You got any Brown's Mule on you?"

"Ah don't go to the privy without hit." Elmo handed over the tobacco, and Dave bit into it.

"Twist her."

Dave tore off the chew and returned the plug. "When do you spit?"

"You'll know."

They delivered the first three loads in good time. Elmo's form had not improved; his legs were probably covered with bruises where the ice bounced against them. But iceman and helper were learning to work together. The sun came out beautifully, there was a south breeze, and tobacco juice flew from either side of the truck. When Dave's curiosity about Hazel got the best of him, he said, "T-Bone, I got some place to go, so I'll leave you with Jiggs."

"Suits me."

Dave was amazed at how well things went when a man was honest.

"The onliest thing, could I kind of drive her up?" Elmo asked.

It was a warning Dave would not have ignored at another time, but he stopped and let Elmo slide behind the wheel. When they reached the cafe Elmo dismounted slowly, hitting the horn button as if by accident. Dave would have been angry, but Jiggs' nickelodeon was so loud nobody heard Elmo honk or saw him get out.

As Dave drove away he began to be excited about Hazel. He breezed past her place a little after nine, going fast in case she ran out into the street to stop him. There was no Acme card in the window and no sign of life at her house. Even so, Dave believed she was watching. He made a U-turn and sped away. He had no special plans, but Elmo had to be used to being dropped somewhere every morning. Dave would want to be with Sue, and if Hazel ever straightened out, he might see her sometimes. He had some eggs and bacon at the Eatwell and heard Theo's latest thinking on John Henry. Sue was not due until noon.

On the last load they stopped at McGrew's First and Last Chance; Dave bought RC Colas and peanut patties and they sat on the bench under the big oak tree. Wartime inflation had played hell with the nickel peanut pattie, which was volleyball-size during the depression when they were called Hopkins County plate lunches. "How come you to hire out at Friendly?" Dave asked, oozing good will.

"Well, muh boy was off soldierin, and the hay baler broke down and I couldn't get parts for hit or anythang else. Everythang come down on muh ears. So I'm farmin what I kin and makin some cash money here. After the war, muh boy and me can commence again."

Everyone had plans that depended on the end of the war. "George — he's my brother — and me might buy a farm. We got a bunch of businesses we are thinking about. If we farmed you could give us some good advice." Chewing tobacco made lots of difference in the taste of peanut patties.

At the next stop they learned about Mrs. O'Konski's accident. Dave was showing Elmo how to get a fifty into her miserable icebox and was assuming Elmo was paying attention when the helper said, "How come you're gimpin around?"

83

"I stepped on a nail," Mrs. O'Konski whined.

Dave sighed. "Okay Elmo, you are going to be on your own one day and you won't know nothing."

Mrs. O'Konski, close to tears, kicked off a tan houseshoe with an Indian face painted on the toe and held out her foot. Elmo hunkered down for a close inspection; the hooks, dangling from his hip pocket, rattled on the linoleum. "You shore did," he announced.

Dave slammed the lid hard, trying to shock Elmo into realizing the jam he would find himself in because of his inattention.

"That there chicken-eatin dog from next door come up and run off with the paper." Mrs. O'Konski's huge, oval face was minus two lower front teeth. "I took out after him and there was this board with a nail in it."

Elmo said, "I used to always step on stobs and such and Ma would wrop up my foot in a coal oil rag."

Mrs. O'Konski's fingers were laced beneath her thigh for support; apparently she intended to show the foot as long as there were any viewers. When she looked up at him Dave felt an obligation to check the foot. He moved in behind Elmo; he had never seen uglier legs. Dave wondered about her husband, who was stationed at Camp Norris; big women like her usually got mixed up with men Elmo's size.

"She ought to have a tetanus shot, T-Bone," Dave said without considering the consequences.

"Tetanus!" Mrs. O'Konski's eyes got big and her face went white. She brought her foot down and scooted it across the linoleum searching for the houseshoe. "What's tetanus?"

"Lockjaw," Dave answered in a comforting tone.

"Lockjaw!" she screamed, scaring Dave badly. She started bawling.

Elmo patted her fat hand. "Maybe you won't be took with it. Me and David hasn't and we have stuck lots of nails in our feet." Mrs. O'Konski sobbed while Elmo worked on her hand and made signs for Dave to say something cheerful. "Hasn't we, David?"

"Yes, I never have caught lockjaw, and I stepped on my first nail when I was three. And I don't know anybody who has lockjaw." She could be heard clear out to the street, and Dave was not crazy about the neighbors thinking he and Elmo were doing something to her. John Henry read the *Police Gazette* and he said fat women were always claiming they got raped by young guys; he claimed he would not deliver ice to any overweight females.

Then Elmo forgot himself and said, "I knew somebody as had it, and they died."

Dave was appalled, as was Elmo himself, who stepped up the tempo of his hand-patting as Mrs. O'Konski wailed for awhile and then settled into steady bellering. She insisted on getting a tetanus shot, but her husband had the car — which was just as well since she could not drive — and she was fighting with her only neighbor. Dave was her only hope; finally he promised to take her to the doctor after they finished the route. Elmo advised her to keep still until then so the poison would not reach her heart.

When they returned, Mrs. O'Konski was ready. She wore a red, floppy-brimmed hat and an orange-flowered dress that she had bought before she gained the last weight. She handed her purse to Elmo and leaned on his arm as they took her to the truck. Since the cab would not accomodate all of them, Elmo stood in the truck bed with his elbows on the roof. Mrs. O'Konski had only the chin quivers until they neared the doctor's office. Then she became hysterical, frightening Dave. "It ain't gonna hurt," he kept yelling over her lamentation. If an ambulance came by, he would sure get rid of a rider, even if it cost him five dollars.

Dave parked in a loading zone and surveyed the steep stairway leading to the doctor's office above the paint store. They unloaded Mrs. O'Konski and, with difficulty, stood her up. Dave got her purse. They draped her arms around their shoulders and started up the narrow stairs;

she did not help much, and Dave was afraid she was going to faint. Both he and Elmo were winded by the time they reached the reception room. Dr. Williams directed them to put her on the examining table. They stumbled back to the waiting room, gasping for air.

"That is one heavy woman," Dave said between breaths. He was sick at his stomach from swallowing some Brown's Mule.

"Oh me," the helper said. He stopped fanning with his hat long enough to raise his sleeve and examine his arm. "And a grip like a monkey wrench."

Dave walked about the reception room, blowing; he had felt better than this after running wind sprints. He decided to sneak out, let some taxicab driver have the pleasure of taking Mrs. O'Konski home. She really was not their responsibility. If they got into the habit of hauling customers around, no telling where it would all end. He was just about to leave when he looked at Elmo; suddenly he knew the helper was thinking the same thing. Each glanced away from the other, embarrassed and reconciled to waiting for their customer.

Mrs. O'Konski was re-delivered in worse shape than before. Halfway down the stairs Dave thought they would never make it. He wished they had gotten a stretcher or made a packsaddle with their arms or lowered her from a window by rope and pulley. Elmo was making desperate sounds. Although he knew better, Dave had taken another chew in the doctor's office; he got rid of it now, spattering the floppy hat, which Dave was carrying. Elmo had her purse. Miraculously, they reached the bottom. They staggered across the sidewalk with Mrs. O'Konski listing to Elmo's side since she was taller than he was. They loaded her into the truck and Dave put the purse and hat in her lap. The helper collapsed on the running board, fanning himself, while Dave leaned on the fender, his head drooping and spattering sweat onto the orange paint. Dave ignored the crowd that had gathered on the sidewalk. He

86

was waiting for the stitch to leave his side when he looked up and saw a familiar face with a gold-toothed smile. Dave tried to grin.

Grandpa said, "You runnin a ambulance now?"

"No sir." Dave started to explain, but lost his temper with Elmo, whose nosiness had caused all the trouble, and everyone with nothing better to do than stand on street corners and gawk at people helping people get tetanus shots. He was too angry to talk. "I got to get her home, Grandpa." He ordered the reluctant Elmo into the truck; the helper threw himself down on the sun-bleached tarpaulin.

All the way home Mrs. O'Konski insisted that they stay with her until the sergeant came in. Dave refused; he did not budge an inch when she reverted to the heavy crying. Instead, he got the next-door neighbor, with whom she had been fighting, to tend her. As they drove away Elmo glanced back. "Lord a mercy I don't want into nothin like that no more."

Rage swept over Dave again. If Elmo had been attending to his teachings on the O'Konski icebox he would have had no foot inspection time. "From here on Elmo, by damn, if they ask you to look at anything, don't look." He thought he would feel better if he could just hit the helper.

Elmo nodded and passed the Brown's Mule.

———————————

Dave came home, still shaken by the O'Konski experience, and found two letters from George. One was for him; the other he could read to the family. The personal letter told about England and how the British treated them, then said:

"I write you, little brother, because there is no one else I can tell how it is with me. The folks and Mary would worry, and I do enough for all of us.

"To make it short, I get scared now. You have to go

through it to understand. On the early missions you are nervous, but the bird takes you there and brings you back. Then you decide nothing can happen; you see the flak and feel pieces hitting the plane, but you are safe. Then some friends, with every bit as good a chance as you, die. You get tired and afraid, and that makes bad luck.

"I am saying, little brother, that I barely got home last night. My gunner was shot through the chest and died this morning. My co-pilot was killed where he sat. I haven't been able to say their names."

He had been writing in ink; now he changed to pencil.

"I will tell you all about this one day, and maybe you will understand, even though Texas is another world. I remember the courthouse fire and my other scrapes and wish I could trade my present troubles for those.

"You are old enough to talk to. And I know you won't repeat this, but the upstairs fire at the courthouse that nobody could figure out, well it was me up there smoking. A bunch of absentee ballots caught fire, and as I was climbing on a stack of old furniture to get a rug to smother the fire with I knocked over one of those things judges sit behind. It must of weighed 700 tons, and it pinned me.

"You remember I had that skinned place on my forehead that I said was from touch football?

"Anyhow, I guess I would have gotten burned pretty bad except for Archer. And you can imagine how Dad would have acted. Archer got me out just in time; we weren't hardly off the square when here came the fire trucks.

"You are probably wearing all my clothes. Just don't go stealing my girl. Ha. Ha."

Long after Dave folded the letter into a small square and shoved it inside his hollow bedstead the words kept coming back. He left the other letter open on the mantel where everyone would notice. He lay down on the floor with the sofa cushion, but sleep was impossible. Once he went into the bathroom and tried to cry, but he could not even do that.

In the end Dave went swimming. He needed sun so his body would match his brown arms and calves. At the pool everyone seemed young and carefree. He retreated as Porky tried to involve him in a scuffle with two Dyersburg farm girls. He wanted nothing to do with any girl. He wanted only to lie in the sun and think about Sue. Occasionally there was a shriek or splash and Porky's laugh as he tickled someone. John Henry arrived with Patsy and Shirley. The girls were glad to see him until he made up an excuse for that night.

"You don't either have to go see your grandmother," John Henry charged.

The girls stared off toward the north.

"Hell, Slicker, I guess I know when I have to go visit my grandparents," Dave tried to sound put upon. Then, to old Shirley's back he said, "I heard that was a good show, though, that you all are going to see and which I hate to miss."

"If you don't want to go, just say so," John Henry demanded.

"Leave him alone," Shirley said.

"He thinks he's so damn much," Patsy added.

Dave felt bad about disappointing Shirley but he was glad Patsy was aggravated. He never had understood how the slicker stood her. "Besides wishing I could go with you all, John Wayne is my favorite actor," Dave said. He reached out and touched Shirley; she stiffened her back without looking at him. "But the whole family has planned this for weeks, especially Ellis, who I try not to never disappoint."

"Hah," John Henry snarled, "I'm going to watch what happens at the Eatwell tonight."

Dave lost his head and pitched John Henry into the water and got called a son-of-a-bitch. After that nobody would talk to Dave, so he swam the length of the pool six times and went home.

Most of the evening he spent with the family. He played kitchen table ping pong and let Ellis win. Mother told how her people came to the Indian Territory, and Dad said the Tottens had been in Wake County a hundred years.

"We came here during the Republic?" Dave asked.

Dad nodded. "Sam Houston was in his second term."

Dave had never heard Dad talk about the past before, although Mother was forever telling about when she was a girl and how it was in her grandmother's time. Her blue eyes would sparkle as she remembered, which usually caused Dad to say, "Vivian, there's no sense in going on about those dead and done times."

But tonight was different, and Dave genuinely hated to leave when it was time to get Sue. "I want to find out all that stuff, but I really got to go now." Dave kept his eyes off his father; people were always making him feel guilty and selfish.

"Let's play some more." Ellis' socks were down so far that, in places, they were not visible above his shoe tops. His laces were untied; the metal tips had been walked off long ago.

"Maybe tomorrow." Dave grabbed Ellis by the nape of the neck and rousted him around. "If you won't feed Dinty anymore peanut butter."

Dad said nothing when he left, but Dave was troubled all the way to the ice plant. He checked the phone messages; someone had used a hard lead pencil, and the naked bulb hanging from the ceiling did not help much. He held the scraps of adding machine paper close. Three calls were from Hazel; they simply asked him to phone 352, which was disappointing. The invented baby, the threats, the mashed butter lie, had reflected a degree of panic that Dave hoped still existed. Maybe he would call her tomorrow; he might never find some of her qualities in

90

Sue. If Hazel were single he would probably be in love with her.

Cedric's entry interrupted his reverie. He sat down and reared back against the wall in a cane-bottomed chair. "Hotshot, you are going to get your tail shot full of holes."

Dave wadded up the phone messages and started to frame a smart answer. Except for throwing ice picks at watermelons and not taking any ice to Hazel — which was justified, if the truth were known — his conscience was clear. But something made Dave hold his tongue. "How come?"

"I mean you're going to get lead poisoned."

Dave stared at the manager, who was not smirking.

"All I know is that along about six a soldier drives up, and O. P. runs out to wait on him. But he wants to talk to the boss, so I go out. And I never seen anybody so mad. He says do I know you, and I says yes, and he says he's going to beat you to a raw pulp."

Dave swallowed hard. "You're kidding."

"I was so surprised I didn't remember everything, but it had to do with his wife, and I think he was mad at Elmo, too, but the only name he ever called was yours."

"That treacherous, black-headed bitch," Dave exclaimed, understanding why Hazel had toned down her phone calls. She was afraid Ted would run into all that sick baby and hot milk crap, which would show her up for the liar she was. Dave could not imagine what Hazel had told, but it sounded like more than hugging and pancake eating. "What did he say?"

Cedric's manner was grave. "I swear to God, Hotshot, I swear he said, 'my wife's all swole up'."

Dave sucked air. He fell back into the swivel chair; the world had turned and bitten him. "Ced, all I did was eat bacon and eggs." In his innocence he searched for an answer, "Maybe it was the milkman? Or the meter reader?"

"Maybe." Cedric crossed his legs and became thoughtful. "You only been here a month, come to think of it."

"Ced, I didn't do a form thing."

"Hell, Hotshot, I believe you."

"Did he say his name was Ted?"

Cedric shrugged. "He said you and the helper would know. I told him Elmo sure hadn't had time to cause any visible trouble. You had to be his man."

"Swell, Ced." Dave threw an ice pick at the wall above Daddy Warbucks' desk. He was almost as angry at the manager as he was at Hazel. A woman that would lie on a man like that was not worth shooting. "You didn't say anything to Mr. Blackstone?"

"No, and it's been years since we generated any," Cedric's eyes widened and the beginnings of a smirk disappeared, "pregnancies." He made a prayerful gesture with his hands. "Hotshot, you didn't?"

Dave fought the impulse to kneel and beg for belief. "No, Ced. I never have. In my whole life. Ask the slicker."

A customer stopped out front and honked. Cedric motioned for him to wait. He touched Dave's shoulder and said, "Anything I can do, Hotshot, I will."

Dave went over the brine tanks and past the machinery to the back lot and sat in the truck. It smelled of sweat and tobacco. After awhile he decided some extra trouble would made no difference, so he started the truck, drove around the building, and turned onto Kentuckytown. Cedric did not seem surprised, in spite of Friendly's truck rules.

Dave had half an hour to kill. His mind kept racing ahead; Ted might be waiting anywhere with an army pistol. Dave had not been so nervous since he dumped black airplane enamel down Nick Clark's tuba. He had calmed himself then by running laps, which was impossible now since it was too late to get cleaned up before Sue got off work.

He drove out to Hazel's house and found the lights off and Ted's car gone, which was unsettling. Dave went down

Garrett Street, past the funeral home and the corner where old lady Badgett pistol-whipped her son-in-law and stopped at the practice field next to the green plank stadium. The cinder track around the goal posts measured a quarter mile. He jogged an easy lap and perched on the truck fender, not breathing hard but sweating entirely too much. A car with one headlight passed, and Dave tried to appear natural sitting on an ice truck at night in a football practice field.

Dave should have made Cedric describe the soldier. He had never seen Ted, but he could recognize him from the strip of brown penny-arcade-machine pictures on Hazel's dresser. Dave had gotten peeved about Ted having his arm around Hazel in one and her wearing his army cap in another. Ted might be searching for him now. There was no limit to the lies Hazel had probably told him. Maybe Ted had beaten her up; Dave would whip him if he hurt her, in spite of the wrongs Hazel had done him.

Dave's shirt was in awful shape. He took it off and waved it around in the dry air, worried about meeting Sue's folks and getting shot. Finally he said to the world, "I didn't do nothing but spend money on eggs and sugar, most of which they ate."

He put on the wet shirt, drove slowly four times around the track, thought how the old Ford, doing laps, must look to someone passing and felt much better.

Sue was as pleased as if Dave had called for her in a Packard instead of a Friendly ice truck. Since Daddy Warbucks lived in south Lawton and he did not know exactly where, Dave made a great loop along the seldom traveled streets and country roads. He stayed well down-wind from Sue and kept in the air stream to dry out. He told Sue about taking care of Mrs. O'Konski, but had to exaggerate — actually, to lie — when he came to the part about her gratitude, which was necessary to make the story good. In fact, Dave had never seen anyone so ungrateful. She did not thank them and threatened to get them fired for not staying until her husband got home.

"This is so nice," Sue said, gazing through the dark at a pasture, "just riding around the country."

Dave stuck his foot out on the running board. "I figured you hadn't seen anything except the middle of town."

She pressed his free hand to her lips. "Thank you for thinking of it."

They were on a gravel road that needed grading. Dave was watching Sue when suddenly the truck fell into a deep and ancient rut, throwing her into the dashboard. Dave jerked his hand away and brought his foot inside as he regained control.

"Are you okay?"

"Yes." She acted as if she wanted to come closer, but Dave kept her away and hoped the shirt would dry. They toured several more miles of rough country road and came back into town from the west. Dave pulled into Sue's driveway and stopped well away from the street in case Mr. Blackstone happened along. Dave rushed around and opened her door, holding his arms out and hoping the slight breeze would dry the wet places. She was at the porch when she noticed him lagging behind. "Come on. Don't worry, they'll like you."

He stalled another couple of minutes and followed her inside with his arms held away from his body like some small-time wrestler.

6

Dave was especially kind to everyone all day. A threat against a man's life gentled him, either because he wanted help when the time came or hoped to be remembered favorably in death. George's letter had affected him too; Dave was grateful to Archer, whoever he was. And caring about Sue made him care about everyone.

Hazel called twice during the day. Setting Dave and Ted against each other had not kept her awake; the first call did not come in until eleven. There was some excitement over the discovery of an escaped German prisoner of war working at the Maddox Mule Barn. Since he did all his talking by hand and was not in the army, Maddox assumed the man was mute. He was a good worker, and all had gone well. Dave saw him almost every time he made his delivery. When the sale started after lunch, the dummy led a mare into the plowed-up ring. Shorty Hall's kid shot a cap pistol and when the horse shied she stepped on the dummy's foot. The dummy swore in pure German.

John Henry just had to go look at him.

"You have seen him around the mule barn."

"But I thought he was just a dummy and didn't pay any attention."

"Slicker, those guys are always escaping."

"But you never get to see a recaptured one." John

Henry's eyes were big and he could not sit still. "He had on civilian clothes, and *Collier's* magazine said prisoners could be shot for spies if they changed out of their uniforms."

"We don't never shoot them." Dave snorted. Then he realized he was being unkind and went to the mule barn. John Henry made a big thing of seeing the prisoner, although to Dave he just looked like somebody sitting in the back seat of a police car wearing handcuffs.

All the way back to the plant John Henry talked about his love for old Patsy; if Dave had not known her he would have thought Patsy was a halfway decent human being from the way the slicker told it. As soon as he could leave without hurting John Henry's feelings, Dave went home.

When he came in, Mother called from the kitchen that there was a letter from George on the mantel. It was addressed to Mother and Dad and had been written the day after the one Dave stuffed up the bedstead, which was more writing than George usually did in two months. Dave took the letter into the kitchen. Mother looked up from the cake she was icing and watched him adjust his scabbard and sit down at the dinette table. "Did you work hard today?"

"We took an extra load to the camp. They aren't happy with Acme." The flimsy envelope had "Free" written where the stamp should be. It was aways strange to get letters from George; people who were close should just know, without anything written down, how things were with each other.

Ellis, barefoot, came in wearing an army helmet liner that fit so low he had to tilt his head to see anyone. "We got a letter from George. Can I take some eats out?"

Mother held the cookie jar. Ellis grabbed a handful and left. "Don't slam the . . . ." she called just as the screen banged shut.

Dave read the letter slowly; its tone was not at all the

96

same as the other. Apparently George had had a bad day when he wrote Dave, but he was all right now. He was flying almost daily and was tired, but he was seeing places that would have remained only names in books. Mickey Farr came over from his base, and they talked about home; Mother was to tell the Farrs that George and Mickey had a good visit. He missed everyone and hoped they saw a lot of Mary, he bet neither Dinty nor Ellis would know him when he got home, he bet Dave was using his good hair grease, and he loved them all. Dave cut his eyes toward the ceiling and swallowed hard. "Sounds like he's doin okay."

Mother's back was to him. "He's well." Her voice broke as she added, "He has a warm place to sleep."

Dave tried to swallow away the lump. It was not safe to look away from the ceiling. The only sound in the room was her spoon scraping the stewer.

"Do you want to lick the pan?"

Dave was relieved to find he was not going to cry. "Yes, ma'am."

She put the pan and spoon aside, still facing the window. Dave walked over to the sink and put his arm around her shoulders. "Nothing is going to happen."

She bowed her head. "Almost every night now the paper has one or two dead or missing."

He took the pan back to the table. "I wonder if we could have Mary over here Sunday?"

She tried to brace up. "Why, I think so. Is the little Greek girl coming?"

"Yes, ma'am, but I found out she's not Greek."

"That's nice." She untied the apron and put it on the drainboard. Keeping her face averted, she went out. She was crying, and Dave did not know anything to do about it.

Dave took his time with the icing. She always left just enough to make it barely worthwhile. After he finished he ran water into the pan and went into the living room to take a nap. When sleep came he was wishing George could be taken prisoner. The treatment would be bad, but he would live.

Dave awoke thinking of George and knowing he had not slept long. George and Sue would like each other; maybe Sue would like George more than him. The thought came before he could stop it, and he raged at himself. Something was terribly wrong with a person who could think such things. He washed his face and rode his bicycle over to Grandpa's. He coasted around to the back yard, kicked the stand down, and dropped, cross-legged, in the grass before the swing where Grandpa sat, bareheaded, and with his sleeves rolled up. "Where's Grandma?"

"Inside. She'll be along." The old man put down his newspaper and grinned, showing the gold tooth. "What happened yesterday?"

"Aw hell, Grandpa," Dave said, before he thought.

The old man laughed and slapped his knee.

Dave went ahead with greater care. "She's a customer that needed a tetanus shot."

Grandma came out the back door wearing a slat bonnet and an apron and carrying a pan of green beans. "Now what are you doing here?" she demanded as Dave pecked at her cheek. She sat at the table next to the tree and took off the bonnet.

"Katie." Grandpa always talked louder to her than to anyone else although she had no hearing problem. "They were carrying that woman over to get a lockjaw shot."

Grandma seemed confused so he increased his volume. "You know. Yesterday."

"Oh." She dumped the beans into her apron and began snapping and stringing them. "Is she all right?"

"Probably. I don't know. She only takes every other day." Dave chunked the ice pick into the ground. It was cool beneath the tree.

"Those injections can make a body awful sick." The corners of Grandma's mouth turned down and she wagged her head.

"Well, old Dave was taking care of the lame and the halt when I saw him." Grandpa laughed and swatted at him with the rolled-up paper.

"Always be good to folks," Grandma urged. Settling into the chair and leveling down on the beans, she was about to give all sorts of warnings and advice, so Dave spoke quickly. "You think you ought to get your grass mowed?"

"How much will it cost?" Grandpa asked.

"Nothin, I need the exercise and sun."

"I guess it ought to get mowed then."

"You'll perish of the sunstroke," Grandma warned.

Dave went into the old shed that had been built when Dad was a boy. It smelled of damp burlap and potatoes and the onions which hung from the roof. He rolled out the ancient mower; Grandpa kept it sharpened and adjusted to a fare-thee-well. He peeled off his shirt and began with the front yard. The grass had a good, moist smell. It itched whenever a piece landed on bare skin. Grandpa owned a catcher, but would not use it. He claimed the dead grass put vitamins back into the ground. But Dave thought mowing was to make the yard look better, and dead yellow grass did not help. Otherwise he and Grandpa agreed on everything.

Dave flexed his muscles and sucked in his stomach. He cut in squares today; sometimes Grandpa's mower made him feel so good he did figure-eights and all kinds of fancy cuts. Everytime Dave had his mower in decent condition, Ellis ran it over every rock and tin can and bottle within a block of the tree house.

Mowing gave a man a chance to think. Dave still did not know exactly what Ted said. He kept wanting to ask Cedric, but John Henry was always around. John Henry was not only naturally nosey, and malicious to boot, but he was still trying to promote old Shirley. Being kind to him all day was hard; he whined constantly about Shirley being on his hands. Last night he had to take out both of them since Patsy was staying with Shirley, which curtailed his romancing with Patsy.

The side yards required only a few swipes. As he started on the back Grandpa called him over. Dave straddled a chair backwards.

"David," Grandma said, "do you lift those big hunks of ice?"

"Yes, ma'am. That's how they get in the houses." Dave was ashamed of the smart answer, but questions like that made him feel like a child. Anyway, Grandma never listened to replies; she was already working on the next hazard.

Grandpa grinned.

"I seen many a young man ruin his self for life over liftin." Grandma never took her eyes off the beans she was stringing.

"Yes, ma'am. I'm careful."

"Grandpa, how long have we been in Wake County?"

The old man fiddled with the red and gold Masonic watch fob and looked at the sky. "Well, my grampa come here as a boy in 1841. So figure it out."

"A hundred and three years."

With his thumb Grandpa lifted his glasses off the bridge of his nose. "Just about. We been here long enough to vote."

Dave was glad he had come.

"Grampa, that was Mamma's pa, fought Yankees and Comanches and skeeters. His pa was the first county judge here."

Dave wanted to tell Sue all this. She would be impressed. He knew very little history, but he thought Oregon had been settled only a short time, and very few people lived there till yet.

Grandpa, with one foot up in the swing, gazed into space. "This was empty country. You didn't have close neighbors. Uncle Nat used to tell how lonesome they got, how as a boy he would sit by the road and hope somebody would

100

come along. It didn't make no never mind that he didn't know them. He just wanted to see people. And maybe he would wait there three or four days hand running and sit ten or twelve hours a day. Not a living soul would pass."

Dave rested his chin on his arms, folded across the chair back. Off toward the roundhouse a train was whistling out. Grandpa consulted his watch and seemed reassured.

It was Dave's third night to take Sue home, and he was waiting inside the cafe. She must have said something, because everyone seemed to know he was waiting for her; Theo did not bother him, nor did Hilda offer a menu. He no longer worried much about the soldiers. Sue's company, after ten o'clock, belonged to him. He kept forgetting what she was like and had to look at her. Sometimes she caught him. Last night he had met her folks, and they acted as if they had always known him. It was hard to imagine her father slamming those doors the first time.

When they left the cafe Theo shook Dave's hand and bade him an almost formal farewell. They had walked far enough for Dave to summarize his day and for her to tell about the fire Hilda started in the deep fryer when Dave asked what he had been wondering about all day. "Your folks think I was okay?"

"Uh huh." She squeezed his hand and smiled.

Dave was sorry he had asked. Now she thought he cared what people said about him, which was not the case. But the harm was done, so he set a leisurely pace, in the event she wanted to repeat all the compliments. "I liked them, too."

She got back on Hilda's grease fire, which really had not been very interesting the first time. After the story had run its course Dave asked, "How old is your dad, anyway?"

101

She did not know. "Hilda isn't a Greek name, is it?" she asked.

Dave thought Hilda was probably German. "What about your mother. How old is she?"

Sue had no idea.

"They look a lot younger than they probably really are."

"I'll tell them."

"Well, I like them, anyhow." It was hard to fish without being obvious.

Sue dropped his hand and put her arm around his waist. He stopped walking, irritated. She came in close, but he would not bend and kiss her. She said, "They loved you."

He turned away, as if he had not heard, and dragged her along. "That's the Carnegie Public Library." He motioned with his thumb.

She ducked beneath a hedge that extended over the sidewalk. "Mother said you were very nice looking."

She was laughing at him, and he did not know what to do about it. "That's the Presbyterian Church over there."

"And Daddy said you acted like you had some brains, which was more than he could say for my other friends."

"That next door house is the Presbyterian parsonage."

She tugged on his arm. "And down the street is where old so-and-so lived."

Dave would not look because he knew she was gloating. "Old Steve Turner," he said.

"I'm not going to tell you one other thing they said," she added in the same infuriating tone.

They walked for awhile, barely holding fingers. Dave was studying sidewalk cracks. "Why?" he asked.

"Why what?"

"Why won't you tell me?"

"Because you're dying for me to, but you don't want me to know it."

"I am not dying for you to do anything," he snapped. "Whenever I want to know anything, Sister, I come right out and ask it." Still unable to look at her, he let her hand

102

go and groped in his pocket, as if he were trying to find something.

"You were driving at it," she said.

Her attitude was better. Dave knew that when he was not certain what to do his best course was to lose his temper. "I don't just drive at things. I don't play guessing games. I was just passing the time of day." There was nothing in his pocket but two quarters and a good-luck marble, but he kept searching.

"I was probably mistaken," she said softly.

He had not won, but he had improved the situation. He waited twenty sidewalk cracks before taking her hand again. Later he would break her from calling Oregon "back home," and he would learn about the boys her father had mentioned. She moved in and he put his arm around her.

"Mother came in and sat on the edge of the bed last night. Her hair was up, and the moonlight came through the window. She talked about going with Daddy. And she cried."

"How come?"

"She's scared for him to go overseas." She leaned her head against Dave's chest. "She wanted to know how I felt about you."

"What did you say?"

"That I wasn't sure. She said it worked that way, that there was always a time when you weren't certain. But if there wasn't going to be anything, you never wondered."

Dave had never known anyone as open as she was. She looked past his chest and said, "There's what's-his-name's house."

"Steve Turner."

"Let's sit on his porch."

They ran across the street and were halfway up the sidewalk when he said, "Naw, we'll save that for a special time." They turned back.

103

"Special like what?"

"Fourth of July. Halloween. Groundhog day."

"An anniversary?"

"I guess."

"If you can stand me. Can you?" They were angling across the street. "Can you?" she demanded.

He laughed.

She stopped on the center stripe. "I'm not moving until you tell me."

"I'll drag you." He tried to sound put out, but could not hide his pleasure in her.

"Get to dragging then, Buster. I'm standing until you answer." She set her feet wide apart and crossed her arms, looking about as powerful as Minnie Mouse.

Out of the corner of his eye he saw headlights coming. "Okay, I can stand you." Laughing, he grabbed for her.

"How long?" She dodged his hand.

"You're going to get run over." Dave was surprised and sobered; the car was close and coming fast. "Okay, a long time."

"How long?"

"Always. Damn you, Sue." He jerked her off the stripe, and they sprinted for the curb as the car passed. Dave was boiling. "You didn't look a single time."

"At what?"

"The car, that's what. He was riding the stripe. What if I hadn't answered?"

"We would still be there."

"Well, that was the dumbest trick I've seen." The anger made it unnecessary to decide how he ought to act toward her. "Don't you ever pull anything like that again."

They played forty-two with Sue's parents, and Dave started home about midnight. He bought doughnuts, finished them, and was needing something to wipe his fingers on when he saw a car parked in front of the house. Dave looked inside and found John Henry on his back with his mouth ajar and his feet sticking out of the window. Dave amused himself by imagining how John Henry would feel tomorrow if he were left there all night long. The trouble was that John Henry would probably wake up at three o'clock and come in and haul him out of the sack.

John Henry wore grey socks with red piping up the ankles. It was a perfect hot-foot situation, but Dave could not afford that kind of thing since he did some sleeping at the ice house. He shook John Henry's shoulder; the slicker mumbled something, pulled in his feet stiffly, and groped in the floorboard for his shoes. "Get in. The dome light don't work. I got to talk to you."

"About what?" Dave handed over the loafer he had found in the floor.

"I'll tell you when I'm woke up." John Henry started the car.

"I can't be gone long." Dave braced himself against John Henry's take-off, which was bad enough when he was wide awake. He gave the car too much gas, cut the corner short, and jumped the curb. Dave ducked, but his head bumped the roof. He forgot about being kind and gentle. "You settle down and don't run over anything else or let me out."

John Henry gave an anguished look and stepped on the gas as they crossed the High Street wooden bridge.

"I need sleep, Slicker. Where we goin?"

"Dutch Inn."

"Aw come on."

"I been a good friend to you, David. Now you got to be a good friend back while I am despondent."

Despondent was one of John Henry's magazine words. His mother took *True Story*. Dave's hands were still sticky. "You got anything I can wipe my hands on?"

John Henry continued his monologue on despondency.

Dave looked in the glove compartment; the maps were too slick to remove doughnut glaze.

As he felt around the floor he found something soft. He had one hand clean when he realized he was not using a piece of chamois. He was holding a pair of women's panties; he could see by a street light that they were blue, embroidered with flowers. John Henry was too busy talking to notice when Dave hung them on the rearview mirror.

As they came to the Dutch Inn, John Henry made a fast, looping, left turn and skidded to a stop.

Dave stormed, "You are gonna get yourself killed. You didn't even check for cars in back of you."

John Henry was ready to argue when he saw the lingerie. He sat perfectly still for a moment, then grabbed, ripping the seat out and bending the arm that held the mirror. He stuffed the panties inside his shirt.

"Them your skivvies?" Dave asked.

John Henry sat pale and open-mouthed; Dave was afraid he was going to pass out. "Let's get some coffee, Slicker."

As soon as they were inside John Henry went into the men's room. He was still pale and trembling when he returned. His water-soaked hair had been parted carefully. Truck drivers talked and waitresses yelled orders above the loud hillbilly music.

"I ordered you some pie and coffee," Dave said.

"I don't know how those pants . . . ," John Henry began.

"Just tell me your news," Dave interrupted, not interested in getting lied to.

The slicker leaned into his confidential hunch. "Brace yourself."

"I'm braced."

"Okay, here goes then." John Henry's lip curled. "I got drafted."

"You're kidding." Dave, struggling to appear appropriately sad, stared at the stale cracker in the empty sugar bowl.

"I got it today and I only been eighteen a month. And Patsy took it turrible."

"When do you go?"

"Thirty days, maybe, and Patsy and me has got to be married first. And you got to help."

"Sure." Dave turned sideways and put his feet up in

the seat. He had been following the conversation in the next booth ever since they arrived; he would consider John Henry's problem after he learned how that came out. A truck driver was trying to get the waitress to go to Tulsa with him and two other drivers were egging him on.

"Patsy feels turrible despondent, and we're counting on you."

Dave nodded. Darla, the waitress, kept saying, in a way that meant she wanted to be begged, that her husband would not let her go.

John Henry's color was getting better. "You can sign for our wedding license and be my best man and Shirley can be best woman."

"Okay, I'll stand up for you." Dave strained to hear Darla's answer after the driver accused her of being scared.

"You got to sign, too, because Pop thinks I don't know what I'm doing."

Dave nodded again, wishing John Henry would keep quiet until Darla made her decision.

Darla passed carrying a coffee cup. She was pretty beat-up and old, thirty at least, but not bad. Her long hair was dyed and she wore an ankle bracelet. Suddenly Dave realized what the slicker was saying. "I can't sign anything for you. I'm just sixteen years old, and I don't even shave."

John Henry grabbed Dave's arm, his eyes pleading. "If I can figure some way?"

"There ain't no way anybody's going to believe I'm your daddy." Darla returned, adding up the check.

"But if I can figure something?"

"You can't."

"But if I do?"

Dave said finally, "Okay." Then, as if by echo, he heard someone at the next booth say, "Okay." The drivers started for the counter, and Darla hurried past.

"What's up?" John Henry asked.

107

"Be quiet," Dave said.

Darla disappeared behind the partition, then emerged without her apron and carrying a purse. The Tulsa-bound truck driver leaned against the phone booth. Darla said something to the owner, who was mopping off the pie case. "You want what?" he exclaimed loud enough for everyone to look up. "You can't do that."

Darla's hand was out, palm up; she gave no sign of backing down. Finally he counted out some bills to her. She waved, and the other waitresses yelled, "Bye, Darla," over the juke box noise. The truck driver took her arm and they were gone, too early to witness the proprietor's fit when he found she had not cleared the drivers' table.

"What happened?" John Henry demanded.

"Tell you later."

The owner was stacking dirty dishes and swearing. Dave swung his feet down, grinning.

"You agree to sign for me then?"

Dave studied his good friend's face and thought of Patsy's torn-up pants and Darla's Tulsa trip and Sue talking to her mother and felt good toward the world. "Okay, Slicker, you figure a way and I'll be your daddy."

7

It was dark and Dave was still sleepy; he was sitting on
the dock poking scoring machine snow down the neck of a
Grapette bottle when Elmo arrived with his blue Br'er
Rabbit bucket and said, "Hidee."

Dave squinted and stared. "Damn, T-Bone is it really
you?"

"How do you like her?" Elmo spread his hairy arms and
threw out his skinny chest. He wore levis and a barrel-
striped T-shirt like Dave's.

"That is uptown doins," Dave answered. Actually, the
shirt had not thrown him off as much as the hat. The brim
was turned up all the way around and Elmo wore it on the
back of his head like a Dyersburg jellybean. "Put your
dinner away and let's deliver some ice."

Things went well enough on the first load. Elmo wanted
to drive up to Jiggs' Cafe; Dave, against his better judg-
ment, let him do it. Jiggs noticed Elmo's new outfit
right away and said he looked twenty-five years younger.

On the way out of Jiggs' place Dave asked, "Are them
levis fading?"

"Lordy yes. My underdrawers has turned complete blue."

He let Elmo drive to the next stop. Dave was flattered
by the helper's outfit, but he was wary; Elmo damn well
better not show up in trooper's boots. Helpers were helpers

and not icemen. "Don't give her so much gas when you take off or you're liable to lose the load," Dave said.

They bumped across the square at a speed well below the one Dave usually set. Elmo bit into his plug.

After taking care of the downtown filling stations Dave drove by Hazel's house. To his great surprise, she had a brand new card in her window, and it was not one of Acme's; it was a Friendly card. Dave felt his heart start beating faster. Perhaps it was a trap, an ambush.

Elmo said, "I didn't know they took off of us. I never been in there."

"We're not ready to make it yet." Dave glared to keep Elmo from asking why until he could invent a good excuse.

"You're a strange feller," Elmo said, without anger.

"I almost forgot to make the new USO job first." Dave snapped his fingers to give plausibility to his near lapse of memory.

They filled the water barrels for the USO carpenters and Dave left Elmo at Jiggs' place. He had nothing to do, so he cruised the Dyersburg Road wondering about Hazel's new card. Maybe she wanted him to come in and shoot Ted. Then she would expect Dave to marry her since she was widowed. He polished his boot on the levis and stuck it out on the running board, determined not to fall into Hazel's trap. He wanted to visit Sue, but Mrs. Wales might not take kindly to his chewing tobacco. The only other entertainment was the scrap drive and the Keep Fit Club for Officers' Wives workout at the old USO. Shy spent all his breaks watching the fat women exercise, but he had very little taste.

Dave chose the scrap drive. He parked across from the courthouse square, bought milk and cinnamon rolls at Helpy Selfy, and sat on the fender to watch the trucks unload metal objects that had been donated to the war effort. This would probably be the last drive. Wake County was pretty well cleaned of scrap metal. Dave worked in the first two drives; this one had been going only three days, but already the scrap was ten feet high and covered an area as big as a basketball court. A man had to watch his metal properties during a drive or somebody would run off with his hitching post or the motor he was re-building. Two or three bathtubs always showed up in the heap.

The various drives excited Dave. He was always relieved when the huge red thermometer on the sign at the courthouse reached the boiling point. There had been campaigns to sell war bonds, collect blood, save tinfoil, write letters to the wounded, give Bibles to the Chinese, and Dave did not know what all. Even the Keep Fit Club was part of a drive, although fat officers' wives were not as damaging to the war effort as some things.

Dave had always worried about not being in the war; having Sue in his life now made it even more important that he do something, although the need for sixteen year old boys was slight.

Elmo was waiting outside as Dave reached the market square. The T-shirt emphasized the helper's tiny pot belly and spider arms. Elmo insisted upon driving away from the cafe, and Dave let him in spite of strong suspicions that Jiggs was being led to believe that Elmo was the iceman. Later in the day Dave twice found Elmo at the wheel with the engine going. He did not object either time, although he was peeved. When Elmo climbed behind the wheel on the next-to-last load, Dave decided to straighten him out. But suddenly Mr. Blackstone popped out of the office and said, "I'm glad you're giving Elmo some driving experience, David."

"Yes sir." Dave went around and let himself in the helper's door. Elmo, glowing, leaned over the wheel, fed her the gas, eased the clutch out, and made a good turn. Dave could not remember being so angry. He had enough problems without Elmo's getting uppity, which he was fixing to do.

"Muh boy's about two years older 'n you." Elmo sounded as if Dave were a guest.

111

"Shove your boy," Dave said, "you are going too slow."

Elmo looked surprised. His speed had dropped off so much that the truck was loping as they entered the inter section of Kentuckytown and Bonham. Dave started to have him shift down to second. "You better . . .," Dave said, but before he could finish, Elmo had dropped into low and stepped on the gas.

Dave felt the load go before he heard or saw. He shouted for Elmo to brake and was out on the running board when the seven blocks, one after the other, hit the pavement, two thousand pounds of ice breaking and sliding all over the intersection. Dave stepped off the running board swearing. The helper finally got the truck stopped. He peered out of the cab like a turtle. "You lost the whole damned load," Dave cried.

Suddenly the street corners were crowded with gawkers; the least happening always brought out everyone in Wake County. Dave surveyed the mess, deciding how best to get the broken ice loaded. Two boys, one rolling a tire, dodged in and out among the blocks. Dave had Elmo back up to the best preserved three hundred pounder. Elmo came out of the cab, threw his hooks into the block, and almost jerked his arms out of their sockets.

Dave knew he should hold his tongue but he was too angry and embarrassed. "Settle your ass down, Elmo."

The helper still strained at the block.

"You're going to rupture your damn self." Dave knelt and started cutting the block into hundreds.

Elmo backed away, puffing. Traffic was stacking up. "Lordy, look at all them cars."

Dave could not bear to see who was witnessing his hu miliation. "They can't go nowhere till we get this place cleared." Dave was tempted to beat up Elmo, which would make him think twice next time he wanted to show off. "Spread the tarp. And you waste one second and I'll kick hell out of you."

By the time Elmo had the tarpaulin over the cab Dave

was swinging the damaged hundred pounders into the truck bed. The helper did not seem to know what to do.

"Just put em where they were before you dumped em." Sweat had popped out all over Dave. His eyes burned from the salt flowing into them. He was going at the job too fast but he was too conscious of the spectators to slow down. Everyone would think he was the one who had lost the load. Traffic was moving a little on Bonham but Kentucky-town was still closed.

Dave stopped to get his breath, feeling the sun's heat bounce off the red brick pavement, and surveyed the out-lying blocks that had come off the truck first. He rested his hands on his hips and narrowed his eyes to lessen the burning. Dave heard the kids with the tire yelling, and then something hit him from the side and buckled his left leg. He caught himself before he struck the pavement; a dusty tire wobbled a few feet and fell over.

Some of the gawkers laughed, and the two boys took off, rolling the tire before them. Suddenly Dave's anger focused upon the fleeing boys. He searched the pavement for a suitable chunk of ice, wiped his eyes, estimated the distance, and threw as hard as he could. He held his breath as the ice barely missed the tire owner's head and then exulted as it hit the other in the back.

Someone cheered. Dave, turning, saw John Henry coming toward him, his hooks at the ready. They had the inter-section cleared in short order.

Elmo pulled the truck over to the curb. Dave mopped his face with a towel Shirley had left one night when they were supposed to go swimming. He could open his eyes all the way now. A block away on Bonham Street the tire owner stood facing Dave; his buddy sat on the high curb, squawl-ing.

"Little bastard's trying to stir up sympathy," Dave charged.

Elmo and John Henry agreed but stayed out of his way. Instead of being flat and crisp, as it usually was, the tarp

113

was as lumpy and uneven as the load beneath it. John Henry left, and Dave got behind the wheel of the truck. His clothes felt as if he had been in a garden hose fight.

Elmo sat close to the door, trying to escape notice. "Are we agoin back to the plant?"

Dave thundered, "No, this ice is charged out to me. So we're agoin out into the city of Lawton to find idiots stupid enough to buy this rough load." Dave bit a chunk of Days Work and made an illegal left turn to go by where all the crying was going on, afraid that the kid might really be hurt. If one more thing happened to him, he was going to join the marines and get his life simplified.

The boys were already gone by the time he got there. Dave started around the block. As he made the second turn he saw the boys running along the sidewalk chasing the tire. They tore across the intersection as if nothing had happened.

Dave sighed.

"You shore popped him good," Elmo said, currying favor. "I used to could throw a clod like that."

Dave shook his finger at the helper. "You just better hope I can get rid of this stuff."

Elmo swallowed hard. "I don't aim to drive no more till I get my own route."

After awhile Dave said, "It's okay, T-Bone." He felt better.

They were rid of the worst part of the load by the time they got to Mrs. O'Konski's. Elmo was in the back getting a fifty—they had fallen into the habit of Elmo cutting and Dave carrying — when Mrs. O'Konski came outside. She closed the screen door quietly. At first Dave thought it was the faded bathrobe that made her look worse than usual, but as she tiptoed toward the truck, he saw that her face was actually broader. Her eyes were puffy, and her skin had a bad color.

As Elmo dragged the fifty back to the tailgate Mrs. O'Konski put her finger to her lips. "Maybe he," she

114

whispered to Dave as she pointed a fat finger at Elmo, "ought to bring it in."

"Him?" Dave bridled; icemen decided who carried what into where. "How come?"

She put her finger to her lips again. Elmo squatted on the tailgate to hear better.

"What's all the quiet stuff?" Dave demanded. The woman was always trying to run him.

"Ernie's home." She gave the house a reverent nod.

"So what?" Dave began before he remembered the risk of doing unjust things in anger; he was just lucky he had not hit the tire-rolling kid in the wrong place and paralyzed him for life. "He's sick, huh?"

"Or maybe asleep," Elmo said with a wistfulness suggesting a desire to be at home in bed.

She opened her swollen eyes wide. "Didn't your boss tell you?"

"Tell me what?"

"That Ernie was going to kill you."

"Kill who?" Elmo groaned.

Mrs. O'Konski waggled her thumb toward Dave. "Him. Maybe you, too, a little. Mainly him."

Elmo took off the hat and, still squatting with his elbows on his knees, studied the crown.

Dave finally found his voice. "He's the one that come to the plant?"

She shook her head vigorously; tears came, as if they had been jarred loose.

"Why?" Dave started to grab her arm, but stopped; probably the idiot would come out right then and that would be all the evidence he needed to prove whatever he believed. Actually, Dave was ready to fight somebody, win or lose, as hard as things had been. The real reason he had not touched Mrs. O'Konski was that he was not sorry for her anymore.

She blubbered quietly. "That serum busted me out in a rash, and I was swole up to beat the band."

"Lordy, Lordy," Elmo said, examining his hat.

Dave spat some of the Days Work. His hackles were up for the eleven hundredth time that day. "We were trying to help you."

"It don't make no difference." She dabbed at her eyes with a bathrobe lapel. "He better take it in though."

Elmo smiled bleakly. "He was just gonna kill me a little."

Dave stared at Mrs. O'Konski and Elmo, then stormed out, "Sonofabitch," as he grabbed hooks and ice and stalked toward the house. Ignoring her protests, Dave bore down hard with his boot heels as he crossed the porch. He slammed the screen door, rattling the glass figurines on the whatnot shelf.

A tall, angular man in an army undershirt and with an eagle arm tattoo tore away the newspaper covering his face and sat up on the couch. "Are you the iceman?" he demanded.

"Yep." Dave stopped directly in front of him. "And that's the damned ice there dripping on your rug."

Dave waited until O'Konski dropped his eyes, then he stalked into the kitchen, dumped the ice into the box, and tore off a coupon. When he returned, Mrs. O'Konski was cowering near the door and Elmo peered in through the screen.

O'Konski leaned back, scratched, and grinned through a day's growth of beard. "Hot ain't it?" he said.

"Yep," Dave answered without slowing. As he passed Mrs. O'Konski he added, "Your water pan got kicked over."

Elmo jumped aside as Dave flung open the screen. He was firmly in the helper's seat when Dave got in. "Lordy, what a day. I had muh ice pick ready."

Dave laughed, nervously. "Okay, T-Bone, just don't look at no more feet."

Elmo was relieved when Dave took the last load by himself. "I'm just tore up generally," the helper said. "Yesterday I found out that muh boy's in the hospital sommers."

"Is he wounded?"

116

"I can't say. We only had a V-mail from him at a hospital." The hat, with the brim turned up, set squarely on his head.

"You go on and get to feelin better."

The helper departed and Dave went inside, took a slice of the melon he had cut that morning, and returned the balance to its hiding place. He tried for a pose that would look as if he were not eating watermelon in case Daddy Warbucks came in. After he finished the slice he dried his hands on Cedric's jacket.

Dave should have been sorry for the accusations he had made against Hazel, but he still did not trust her. Even so, since she had a new Friendly ice card he thought he might forgive her. Dave recited, all the way to her house, a speech putting a heavy emphasis on her jealousy and bad disposition.

His brakes caught solid for a change, and he skidded in the loose gravel. He hooked a fifty and went inside as if the last few days had not occurred. The front room was all movie magazines and heaped ashtrays. Her bed was unmade, and there were dirty dishes and clothes all over the kitchen. The bathroom door was closed. Dave knocked and called, but there was no answer; Hazel was not there.

Dave leaned back against the sink. There was a sadness, a sense of loss, in her disorder, just as there was in her words and the look out of her eyes. Dave was close to tears, because of her warmth and loneliness and lostness, and because he almost loved her.

He became aware of the ice wetting his levis, and suddenly he was angry because of the mess she made Ted live in and because she was not there. He put the ice in the box and pocketed the money. On the way out he stopped to see what was on the Victrola turntable. She had been playing "I'll Be Seeing You," which he began singing as he drove away; its melody hung in his mind long after he stopped humming it out loud.

"Well, Totten, it's this way," Daddy Warbucks began after raking Dave's twelve cent overage into the cash drawer.

Dave winced; the old man was about to tell him lots of things he could live without knowing. Dave resented the waste of time almost as much as the twelve cent loss.

"I saw you the other evening in a pair of trousers." Mr. Blackstone had the Yankee habit of using evening for night and dinner for supper. "And the next day you had on a different pair."

"Yeah, I got a bunch of 'em."

"Now you look at these." Daddy Warbucks got up and turned so Dave could see the old, baggy, blue trousers from every side. "I have worn them every summer for I don't know how long." He shoved his hands deep into the pockets. "You would not think it, seeing their fine condition."

"Totten, that is the way you find out how good a pair of pants really is. Feel that material."

Dave reached out. The cloth reminded him of his tarp. "Pretty good," Dave lied. Then he noticed Cedric's feet on the tanks; he was listening. One day Dave was going to settle the manager's hash for good.

Mr. Blackstone, pleased, moved his swivel chair closer to Dave. "It is foolishness to have a closet full of clothes. You must wear them out to know how good they are."

A car pulled up and Dave, relieved, started out, but suddenly Cedric streaked onto the apron and loaded a fifty into the car. The old man watched approvingly, but Dave was not fooled. Cedric knew if Dave waited on the customer he would not come back and he knew if Daddy Warbucks went out to the car, Dave would sneak away. Cedric was only trying to prolong the conversation so he could eavesdrop some more, which showed where Warren got some of his sorriness.

"I like to give others the benefit of my experience, Totten, and I have always considered you a splendid sort."

Cedric was fiddling around the cash register. Dave bit into the Days Work, wishing the manager would leave.

"Does Malvin know you do that?"

"No sir."

Daddy Warbucks shuddered. "It is a waste of money and a filthy habit."

"Yes sir."

"Anytime you want to talk some more, stop in." The old man turned to his desk. Dave fairly flew to the melon vault, where Cedric overtook him and smarted off; Dave slandered his mother. Cedric was laughing himself silly, so Dave went to Smalley's Grocery and talked to an old farmer while he ate a peanut pattie.

Later Dave took Sue to the Joshua Pendleton Municipal Park swimming pool. It was her first time there. They sprawled at right angles with their heads close together on the grassy patch at the shallow end. Sue lay on a huge beach towel, the first one Dave had seen in real life, although people in the movies had them. Dave was stretched out on two greyish pieces of terrycloth stencilled "Lawton H. S. Ath. Dept." Missing his nap told on him. "I sure am getting drowsy," he said.

"Sleep some then."

They were as far as possible from the pool, where little kids chased each other up the ladder, yelled, and came off the diving board like frogs. They got into arguments and scuffled, and Perry Sessions, the lifeguard, threatened them constantly.

Dave rested his arm on his forehead. He was nearly asleep when the heat lessened as the sun went behind a cloud. "You like being with me?"

She was quiet.

He thought she had not heard. "Sue?"

"I'm here."

Her voice came from far, far away. "It's natural."

"Why natural?"

"It just seems right."

119

"But why?" The time between questions and answers was so long Dave thought he slept a little each time.

"I don't know," she said angrily. "You make me say things, but you never do."

"I do too," Dave stated, knowing he had never matched her openness. He sat up, and she did, too, which surprised him. Usually she backed down before his anger.

She said, "I just the same as told you I loved you any number of times." Her green eyes were perfectly clear, in spite of the swimming she had done.

"I have, too," Dave shot back without sufficient force to make it work. He looked away. "I just can't talk yet."

"Well, you just quit trying to draw me out then, Buster." She huffed off to the pool and made her dive just past Perry's stand.

Dave wondered if he dared get the slicker to deliver Hazel. She did not live far from his route. He was watching Sue turn at the end of the pool when a familiar voice jarred him. There by the bathhouse was John Henry horsing around with the assistant lifeguard. Dave's heart stopped; the slicker would not be there without Patsy, and Patsy would not leave Shirley at home. Sue was at the deep end, with her back to him.

Dave trotted over to John Henry, who brayed, "Hey, my old buddy."

"Shirley with you?" Dave demanded in a low voice.

"Yeah." He started to call into the girls' bathhouse, but Dave clapped his hand over his mouth. "Just shut up. And keep shut up."

John Henry became sullen as he realized he was not going to get rid of Shirley. "You got that Greek girl here?"

"She is not the only girl I know. Besides, she ain't Greek."

"Well whatever she is, she is about to meet old Shirley. And you and me got to discuss that other matter."

"You had better take good care of me if you want help

on that other matter is all I can say." Dave did not wait for the slicker's answer.

Sue was back at her beach towel. Dave needed to move her quickly without being obvious. He fidgeted as he devised his strategy.

"Do you want to go?" she asked.

"Oh, no. I'm here for the afternoon." Dave sat down to demonstrate a lack of urgency. "Why? You don't have to be some place in the next little while do you?"

Sue studied Dave for what seemed like half an hour, then said, "I guess I should start getting ready for work."

Dave made himself move slowly, although he expected Patsy and Shirley to come out momentarily. He folded the towels and walked Sue toward the bathhouse, resting his free hand on her shoulder and slowing her gait. He exchanged pleasantries with Perry's assistant while he glowered at John Henry to keep him away.

At long last they were at the girls' dressing room. Dave was barely breathing. As Sue went in, Dave scurried for the boys' side. Shirley and Patsy were in there with Sue, which caused Dave some concern; but they would not know each other. Doubtless John Henry had told Patsy about Sue, but Patsy would not venture into Theo's even if she were dying of curiosity and hunger.

Dave held his ear to the wall, trying, without success, to hear what was happening in the girls' side. A little kid with glasses and cotton sticking out of his ears stared as if Dave were doing something perverse. Dave made an unkind remark to the kid and stopped listening.

Dave was in the parking lot sitting on his bicycle when Shirley came out wearing her red two-piece suit. She and Patsy joined John Henry at the grassy place. Dave backed up so they could not see him. Finally Sue arrived. Dave helped her onto the bar and they headed toward town with as much speed as Dave could summon; the afternoon in the sun and water and the loss of sleep had weakened him.

"This girl in there . . . ," Sue began.

Dave almost lost his balance. Sue had been in the bath-house so long because she was plotting with Patsy and Shirley against him. "In where?"

"The bathhouse." She twisted about to face him.

He started pumping so she could not look him in the eye. "She was the loudest human being I have ever seen."

New strength flowed into Dave's legs as it appeared she had nothing else to say. "Who was she?" he asked, to be certain he was safe.

"I don't know, but she had a two-piece red suit."

"Huh," he said, grateful for his deliverance.

That night George came to him in a dream. A little boy was with him who was probably the other Georgie, Dad's brother. Dave awoke weeping, but without tears, and sat out the rest of the night listening to the little radio, afraid to sleep. He was terribly sad but did not know why. Perhaps it was that he did not deserve the good things that were his and because of his slight merit he would have to give up something or someone. And there was no one he could spare; not Sue, not Grandpa, not George, not even Ellis.

When the sun came up all of Dave's sadness and fears disappeared. He vowed to stop being such a baby and decided he would never again eat two cantaloupes at bedtime.

8

As soon as he dropped Elmo for breakfast Dave made a beeline for Hazel's place. She probably had been shocked to find he had been there yesterday. He had a new speech ready. In Bogart's words, it was going to be the kiss-off. He wanted to be able to shoot square with Sue. Dave parked in the shade, in case it took awhile to get her told. The ice card still showed 50 pounds, which was more than she would need. He hooked a twenty-five. The front door was ajar but the screen was latched. He knocked, but there was no response, so he went around to the back. The car was gone, which meant little since Ted sometimes took it.

Dave opened the gate carefully and stooped to pet Hazel's terrier, Alec. As he crossed the yard, Dave held the ice over the dog's face and watched the drippings splash his black nose. Dave moved up the steps to the screened-in porch and found the door latched. Alec lost his footing and fell down the steps, barking hoarsely and thinly. Dave rapped again, with no result. He leaned close but could not hear her inside.

Dave swung out of the backyard, with Alec barking. Hazel had locked him out purposely. She was going to keep him out there until her whim was satisfied and then put on her surprised act. Dave was livid. He pitched hooks and ice onto the tarp and was in the cab when he heard her call and saw her out of the corner of his eye. She was spiffed up and smiling and holding the front door open.

Dave had done nothing to show that he had seen her. He forced himself to wait long enough to take a chew, then he hit the starter. He got a good look at her in the mirror as he turned the corner. She was out on the porch, and her face was sad and hurt. For a moment he considered going back, but he hit a chug hole that pitched him against the ceiling. By the time he finished the load, Hazel was doing the sick baby routine again.

"Now, Ced, I told you that one ain't got no baby." Dave threw his hooks against the sideboard. "Besides, I took her fifty yesterday, and she would of got lots more today if her house wasn't locked. She didn't tell you I went to both doors and her dog bit me." Dave stuck his thumbs into the levi pockets and spat tobacco juice on the driveway.

The plant manager started to smirk. "I begin to see, Hotshot."

Elmo, standing in the truck bed with his hooks dangling from his hip pocket, asked, "What customer is that?"

"Smooth out that tarp," Dave ordered. "It's one you wouldn't know."

Cedric tapped his temple. "I'm getting the picture."

Elmo's voice rose. "I orter know somebody if they are on our route?"

Dave regretted his kindnesses to the hayseed. "Elmo, straighten the damned tarpaulin."

Cedric said, "That was the guy who was going to kill you."

"Oh no. That was O'Konski, wasn't it, Elmo?"

The helper stopped straightening the cover. "Yeah, Sergeant O'Konski."

"And O'Konski lives at 814 Pendleton." Cedric strained like a bird dog around quail."

"No. No. Ain't he wrong, Elmo?"

"That's right," the helper said. "He's wrong."

Cedric was pleased with himself. "Well, something is going on that you don't want looked into, Hotshot, so you better get your business settled before Mr. Blackstone learns about it. If you get my meaning."

Dave spat the Days Work. One day he was going to let some facts slip about Warren. Actually he knew nothing really bad about Warren, but the manager would figure he did. Cedric made him call Hazel and say he was on the way; when he arrived she was perched on the porch railing and was visibly unhappy about Elmo being along. She flounced into the house.

"You want me to take it in?" the helper asked.

"No, but come with me." They found Hazel in the living room smoking a Camel cigarette; Dave was pleased to note her dress had wet arm circles. "Your card said fifty." Dave was sure she could not use that much.

"That's what I want."

Elmo was following close enough to step on Dave's heels, but somewhere along the hall Dave lost him. When Dave found half of yesterday's fifty still in the box there was no one to hand it to. Dave replaced it with the new block and chipped and poked the old ice down by the sides. The lid still would not close, so he put the leftover chunk in the sink. Hazel and Elmo, in a big weather conversation, had drifted back to the kitchen. "You can't leave that ice there," she said.

Dave opened the lid to show that the box was full. "You want it in a paper sack?"

He laughed, but nobody else did.

Hazel was rummaging through a black patent leather purse. She was prettier than Sue, but Dave knew by the way she stood and held her head and talked that she would never belong to anyone very long. She flashed her wedding ring and avoided touching his hand when she paid him.

Dave said, "You can make iced tea with the sink chunk."

"I might have figured that out by myself."

Dave had some suitable retorts, but he preferred not to fight.

"It was kind of you to come. I have only called three dozen times."

She was showing out for Elmo's benefit; Dave was still boiling when he got to the truck. Elmo came out five minutes later even though Dave had raced the motor and done everything but honk to make him hurry. The hick staged a big waving scene; he leaned out his window and watched her until they turned the corner, then said, "I forgot to ask after the baby."

Dave started to answer, then realized Elmo actually believed in the baby. He wondered how anyone could be so simple and be forty-two years old. Dave began calculating how much Friendly had spent delivering that fifty pounds of ice to Hazel; he could use it the next time he got into an argument with Cedric.

"I heard from muh boy. He didn't get wounded."

"Oh?" Dave really did not want to think about Elmo's son. He wished he knew what to do about Hazel. If he traded her, John Henry would probably stumble onto what had been going on, and tell everybody. Hazel might get crazy about the slicker, but that was unlikely. The real hazard was her going over to Acme and getting mixed up with Ace Howard.

"He was in the hospital because he set around on concrete working on airplanes and come down with piles."

"Yeah?" Dave's interest was stirred.

"He wrote that they gave him the Purple Heart."

"Aw."

"I know. That's what I said."

Since it was Saturday Dave sent the helper home early and went down to the Eatwell.

"We have really been busy," Sue said.

Dave leaned on the cigar counter to make everyone aware of his claim to Sue. The cafe was filled with soldiers; of ten thousand on weekend passes, twenty knew what to do. The rest spent their pay on food and candy, loafed on Lawton street corners, complained of being bored, and went back to camp to sleep away the weekend.

"You are still off tonight?"

"Yes." Her eyes sparkled.

"We'll get you about seven."

She reached out and brushed his lips with her fingertips. Dave hoped everyone had seen. Not sure what to do with the rest of the afternoon, he walked a couple of blocks toward the square and then turned north. The sun was still high, and there were no clouds to blunt its thrust. Some kid had abandoned a crumpled tin can and shinney stick at the First Baptist Church. Dave hit the can a few times, keeping it out front of him, then decided he was too old for tin can shinney. He landed a final blow and the can, reflecting the sun, skidded and rattled across the street.

Dave swung the stick as he walked. Not so long ago possession of such a smoothed piece of tree limb would have made it a very fine day indeed. As he passed the junior high he considered pitching the stick up on the roof, but was repelled by the waste. Just north of the school Dave turned in at a house with a window flag. One of the two stars was gold for Mary's older brother, who was the first Wake County casualty.

Dave rapped with the stick. A long time ago he delivered the *Star-Telegram* to this house. Mary was dating George then, but Dave had not really known her. In fact, he had been scared of her since he did not know what to say to girls.

The door opened and Mary threw her arms around him. "Come on in."

"Okay, but I got a bunch of things to do." She hugged him again and he felt sheepish. Dave never knew how to greet women; either they turned a cheek and then withdrew about the time he figured out that he was supposed to kiss it, or they clutched him and acted offended when he hugged back. He had never exchanged any satisfactory

127

greetings with any female except Sue and Hazel and Shirley.

He followed Mary through the cool, dark living room, past George's picture on the bookcase.

"Mother went downtown and Daddy is having the car worked on. Somebody from Dallas sold him a gadget to double his gas mileage."

"Those things don't work."

"I know but Daddy likes to believe they will."

Dave sat at the kitchen table and listened to her and felt bad about seeing her so seldom. He had pitched one cat out of his chair and he saw three others at various times. A cat oversupply always made Dave think of old maids and widow women, but George would fix that. Lots of Mary's cats would get thrown out.

Mary was about twenty-three, not much over five feet tall, and had oversized brown eyes. She smiled in a way that used to make him think she had something on him.

"How's everything at the gas company?" he said.

"Fine. How's everything at the ice plant?"

"Well hell, Mary," he complained as she shrunk his store of conversation material.

"You want to know how many gas customers we have and how much money we get from them?"

He hesitated. "No. Not really."

"Or how about the new franchise agreement with the city?" Her eyes were bright and she was enjoying herself.

"When George marries you my advice is for him not to. Either that or whip your butt."

She clapped her hands and laughed. Finally she took pity on him. "George is proud of you. He writes about you a lot."

Dave's face got red. He wanted to talk about what he and George would do after the war but decided to think on it some more. She gave him lemonade with ice cubes, which pleased Dave. Mary's family had worn out two or three refrigerators before Mother got her Frigidaire. The Tottens

128

always lagged twenty years behind everyone in taking up anything new. Dad talked about Mary's father handling a WPA shovel during the depression and still not knowing the value of a dollar, but Dave admired his style.

"Did Mother ask you over tomorrow?" He shivered as the oscillating fan blew on his damp T-shirt.

"Yes."

"Are you coming?"

"Yes. The folks will have Sunday dinner at the hotel."

"Did Mother say anything else?" Dave tried to sound casual.

She grinned and hunched her shoulders as if they were jacks players. Her eyes were big and round, and she appeared to be about twelve years old. " You mean about the Greek girl?"

"Not necessarily. I just wondered what other topics Mother discussed." He thought he ought to be angry but was not sure of his grounds. "She's not Greek though."

"Oh?"

"No."

"What is she?"

He rubbed the dust off his boots with a handkerchief. "Nothing I guess."

"Do you like her?"

"I guess."

"Are you fighting with her?"

"No."

"Well, what are you doing here?"

Dave realized then, with some shame, that he was always in trouble whenever he visited her. He considered righteous indignation but decided to flatter her instead. "I like your hair ribbons."

"I don't always wear them. Now, what's wrong?"

He wished he could talk about Hazel and Sue, but there was nothing she could say. "Not a thing. Really."

She shrugged. "Okay. I haven't known you most of your life, and I don't have any idea how you operate."

129

Dave let some time pass while he gazed out the window at a bird collecting twigs beneath a peach tree. "George said he saw Mickey Farr."

"Yes," she agreed.

Dave knew that a man thwarted a woman's curiosity at his risk; Mary was going to be tight-mouthed. "Did George say anything to you about starting a taxi company?"

"Gracious, no."

"But he hasn't said he was going to do anything else?"

"No. We never talked about what he'll do."

Dave was relieved. "Well, new cars are going to be so cheap that me and George could put in ten or fifteen cabs."

"Lawton doesn't have enough people."

"Look," Dave said with some impatience, "lots of thought has gone into this and there will be a lot more. The lack of Lawton population is one of the problems we are working with."

Mary studied him with a level gaze he could not translate. "I guess so." She got a little sad when he left. They stopped in the living room at George's picture and she took his hand. For a moment he had a vision of a future without George; she would get smaller and smaller as the years passed and the cats increased.

Dave was glad he had kept the stick. He chopped at the leaves on low hanging branches pretending they were German planes threatening George. He wished Mary and his brother were married; it would give them all a stronger claim on George.

———

They reached the lake right after dark, spread the blankets, and set the eats on the fender of Porky's Buick. Dave and Sue left Porky and Betty and went walking by the water. It was cooler there. Even so, it was still a hot night. Sue wore a white blouse and a full black skirt.

She sat on a log while Dave skipped rocks. "You know," he said, "the first couple of times it hits the water you think it will go on forever."

"Yes."

"And then you feel bad when it goes under." Dave threw half a dozen, each harder than the one before. If he could get enough steam on it the rock would never sink. His shoulder burned and he sat down beside her. For the first time, he was aware of smoke. "That smells good."

She agreed. "But it's sure too hot to cook out tonight."

Dave studied the orange reflection in the sky, alarmed. "That's over by our place."

"Maybe the forest is on fire."

Dave grabbed her hand and they ran toward the flames. As they neared the campsite they saw Porky stoking a bonfire. "How do you like her?" he yelled as flames shot ten feet above the limbs he had piled chest-high between the two blankets.

"Aw hell," Dave complained, as unhappy with himself as with Porky. Nothing ever turned out right when Porky was around, but because of the Buick he kept giving Porky second chances. "We don't have nothing to cook. And if we did, nobody could get close to that thing." Dave shielded his face from the heat and dragged away his blanket.

"I told him not to," Betty said. She sat at the farthest corner of the other blanket.

"Whoever heard of a picnic without a fire," Porky brayed, his forehead glistening in the yellow light.

"That thing is bigger than a car."

"That shows how much you know, Totten. People can cook all around a fire like this."

Dave clenched his fists.

"We can go over there, David." Sue pointed to some high ground a hundred yards away.

"Okay," he said to her for Porky's benefit, "I'm leaving.

131

And if anybody lets a forest fire get out of control it will all be on their head, not mine."

Sue traded for some pickles, and Dave picked up the basket, threw the blanket across his shoulder, and asked, "You people coming?"

"Let's do," Betty pleaded.

"And waste all this!" Porky held his palms to the blaze.

"Adios then. If you get to wanting to act right, let me know." Dave headed for the high spot with Sue following. When he stopped he glanced about, pleased with the site, and spread the blanket. Sue knelt before the basket; she held each item before Dave, named it, and set it on the blanket.

Dave lay back and rested his head on his forearm. "Did you ever study the stars?"

"I had a book about them when I was little and I read it till the pages fell out."

"Sometimes you feel like they're so close." He reached up; then the flames distracted him and his anger returned. "That damned Porky."

"After supper we'll put our heads toward the fire and we won't notice it."

Dave raised up and glared toward the conflagration. Porky was a silhouette strolling back and forth between Betty and the fire with a sandwich and a root beer.

"It will be all right, David."

"That idiot acts like it might go out."

Sue touched his shoulder, and Dave realized she was afraid the picnic would be spoiled. He smiled. "Porky is about the dumbest guy I know. Him and his date usually get to tickling one another." He admired the things she had laid out and said, "Sure looks good."

They had almost forgotten Porky when Betty got there. "Aw, Dave," she wailed in a high, thin voice, "do something about him." She was flushed and her hair was damp.

Dave swore. "It don't look like it's burnt down much."

Betty was about to cry. "My face is blistered."

132

A shower of sparks shot up. "What's he doing?" Dave demanded.

"He says it isn't big enough. He's building it up."

"The hell he is." Dave searched for his loafers around the edge of the blanket. "He's not getting away with this." He stepped into the shoes and loped off across the clearing, trying to cool off; Porky could get the Buick anytime he wanted it.

Dave's conversation with Porky went badly and he took the root beers out of the bucket, poured ice drippings on the fire, and made half a dozen trips to the lake for water. When he was through the fire was considerably diminished, but the smoke was very thick. Porky sulked on his blanket.

Dave warned Porky, "You got all the fire you need, so don't build it up."

Porky turned his back.

"And you keep Betty entertained so she stays out of my hair."

Dave felt like a bully as he went back to Sue.

"Lordy, that sure helped," Betty said.

Dave did not answer. It looked as if she could settle Porky some. Dave was glad when she left. They finished off everything but the cake. At Porky's campsite only a few flames were visible in the smoke. Betty sat motionless by the fire as Porky sprawled on his stomach.

Sue proffered the dessert.

"I just can't now."

"I know."

"I feel pretty mean, but he sure had it coming."

"You could go say something to him, act like you were down there to borrow napkins or something."

Finally he decided to follow Sue's suggestion. He put on his shoes, went down to the clearing, and reached Porky's blanket before he knew what to say. Betty had been watching as he approached. Dave thought she would have the sense to begin a conversation, but he was wrong. He stood there in silence. The wet campfire gave off a heavy odor.

133

Porky ignored him.

Dave picked up a couple of Woosie's root beers that he had thrown out of the ice bucket. He cleaned off the grass and leaves stuck to the bottles. "You got the opener?"

Porky did not move. Betty rummaged in the basket and handed Dave a rusty can opener. He took his time uncapping the bottles, hoping an idea would come; it never did. Dave left them as he found them, with Betty resting her chin on her knees and Porky acting dead.

He was drained when he got back to Sue. He flopped down on the blanket and she turned to him, using his shoulder for a pillow. "I struck out, Sue."

Someone giggled. Sue raised up and looked toward the fire. "Don't feel bad. Porky is tickling her."

By the time they started home Porky was in a good humor. Dave got out at Sue's house. Because the porch swing made too much racket, they sat on the steps. It was good to be with Sue, but Dave was thinking more and more of friends only two years older than he was who were thousands of miles away fighting to stay alive on Pacific islands no one had heard of before the war. He wished he could help George.

"What is Mary like?"

"You'll meet her tomorrow."

"Will they like me?"

"Probably." He sat one step above her, and she leaned her head against his chest. He pointed to a falling star.

"Why didn't George marry her?"

"I don't know. He never went with anybody else. They were always together, and when coaches came about football scholarships they talked to Mary, too."

"I don't see why he didn't marry her."

He was surprised by her anger. "Well, I don't either, Sue, but I don't see . . . ."

She pulled away. "This old business of 'I may get killed and I don't want you hurt,' I say baloney."

134

"Yeah." Dave was not sure what was wrong, but he knew better than to disagree.

"Baloney and baloney and baloney." She looked him in the eye. "If somebody did me that way . . . ."

It seemed that he was being accused of something; when he tried to pull her to him she fought him off.

"Your fat friend, Porky, and the others may not see through you, but I do." She got up and moved out of reach.

"Look, I didn't do nothin. Maybe she turned him down."

"Do you know that for a fact?" she demanded.

"No, by God, I don't. But I don't know that George didn't ask her, either."

Her mouth was pursed in disapproval of his language. "I think you had better go."

"What in the world is wrong?"

The corners of her mouth fluttered and she did not resist when Dave put his arms around her. "What has got into you?"

She put her face against his chest and began to cry. "You never once said you love me."

Dave talked fast. Desperate and running out of material, he told about the courthouse fire. By the time he left she was so curious about Archer that she said nothing about his failure to reply. He had to get the details of the courthouse episode from George because the story he told was mostly lies, since he had more time to fill than facts.

Everything went well Sunday. Grandpa, with his sleeves rolled up to the elbows, talked to Dad about the war, comparing it with the previous one. Sue and Mary hit it off splendidly; they went up to George's room. Dave wished he could hear their conversation and hoped it was about him.

Grandma wore a high-collared black dress pinned with a silver clip. She moved between the kitchen and living room

135

warning everyone but Grandpa of perils; she steered clear of him. She told Dave about sun causing cataracts and thought the blood vessels stood out too far on the back of Dad's hand.

"Katie!" Grandpa said, and she went back to the kitchen. "She hangs around those old cranks down at the church and hunts up the *Reader's Digest* pieces on sickness and reads all the obituaries in both papers and keeps score of the causes of death."

Grandpa shook his head and Dad laughed.

"She's always done that, Papa. You just never noticed until you retired."

"Read me some more, David." Ellis, still wearing his Sunday School clothes, listened to Dave explain the funnies; he read well enough to understand them but preferred having someone else do it.

Dave was preoccupied; if Sue were not there he would be much more interested in Joe Palooka's preparations for the heavyweight championship fight. Actually he did not want to be entertaining Ellis, but it made a good impression on Sue. Then too, if he hung around Sue all day, someone would likely kid him about it. He had taken her to church earlier and as they were going in Porky and Betty arrived in fine fettle. They sat in the pew in front of Dave. While everyone stood and sang, "Oh Lamb of God, I Come, I Come," Dave set an open hymnal under Porky. It was an old Sunday School trick, pulled so regularly that Porky was very careless when he sat without first looking. He came down hard on the corner of the book and cursed. The back of Porky's neck got red; he had been impaled on too many Baptist Training Union songbooks to get upset about the pain, but because of the swearing he would not speak to Dave after church.

An old voice called him back to the present and he said, "Yessum."

"You want to watch that sun," Grandma said. "This time of year is particular bad for the cancer."

136

Dave agreed and turned the page to *Mandrake the Magician*.

Ellis had a skinned face from playing punch the icebox last night. He had tripped over a shovel in the doctor's yard, and landed on the sidewalk. "Lothar is pretty tough," he said.

Dave put his arm around Ellis' shoulders, feeling affection for the little brother in spite of his shortcomings. The dinner was a Christmas kind of event for Dave, a time when the people he really cared about—except for George— were together. Sue and Mary came downstairs and went into the kitchen. Grandpa finished his story; his gold tooth caught the light and he and Dad laughed. Out of conversation, they fell silent and grinned and did not look at each other.

Mary came in, took Dad's hand, and led him up out of the chair. "Mrs. Totten says everything is ready if you'll bring the fan."

Dave quit folding the funny papers and started to get the fan, but Dad waved him off and bent stiffly to pull the plug. Dave had already put the table leaves in and carried chairs from all over the house. Mother directed the seating while Grandma brought the rolls. Ellis, perched on a stool and pleased to be with the grownups, held his head back while Grandma tucked a napkin into his collar. Mother beamed at Ellis and took her place at the foot of the table. When she had assumed an appropriately sober expression, she nodded to Dad.

Dave was the last to bow his head. He held Sue's hand beneath the table as Dad spoke the soft words against the whirring of the fan: ". . . and watch over us and guide us and cause us to be worthy of thy Son. And care for and keep our son and bring him home safe. Soon. Amen."

9

Elmo could not be persuaded to drive the truck now; when Dave insisted, his only answer was to chew with shorter, quicker bites and spit more than usual. "What about when O. P. goes in the army?" Dave demanded as they were returning to Lawton from the camp. Elmo had installed a huge, yellow-flowered pillow on the helper's side after he heard of his son's painful malady, which had resulted from sitting on concrete. He perched squarely on the pillow, staring ahead and giving no sign that he heard. "Huh?" Dave said.

Elmo sighed. "We'll milk that'n when her udder's full."

"But what are you going to do?"

"O. P. ain't gone nowhere."

There was truth in that; O. P. had received another thirty day extension. Suddenly Dave realized O. P. was about to get drafted last summer. In fact, he was on a thirty day delay then.

"Well if one little load-dumping stopped me I wouldn't be where I am today."

Elmo snorted. "It wasn't no little thing then. You turned on me complete."

"I did not turn on you," Dave shouted, shocked by the helper's attitude.

"You did, too," Elmo yelled.

"Did not."

"Did, too."

"Didn't."

"Did."

"Didn't."

Elmo spat into the Folger's coffee can he started using as a spitoon after his door developed a rusty cast. A silence set in that lasted all day.

The following morning Dave came to work early, afraid Elmo might somehow outmaneuver him. Daybreak was still an hour away. He sat in the truck, offended by Elmo's pillow. Then he sprawled across the seat, with his feet out the driver's side and his head on the pillow. He was going to get rid of Hazel today; Sue knew something was wrong and he owed Hazel nothing. Although she had not been out of his mind for a whole hour since they met, what had to be had to be. If she chose to get used and thrown away by Ace Howard it was her hard luck.

Dave dropped off to sleep and dreamed of Hazel. He was awakened by John Henry yelling "Deep in the Heart of Texas" and pounding on the helper's door. Dave called him a son-of-a-bitch, which seemed to make no impression.

John Henry leaned inside the window, all scrubbed and combed. "Listen, you got to get us married."

Dave tried to focus his eyes. "I ain't got to get you nothin."

"It's all worked out."

"And old Shirley is best woman I bet." Dave's eyes burned and his mouth was dry.

"Yep. Damn, I sure am in love."

"Well, I can't afford to get mixed up with old Shirley again." Dave crawled out of the truck and started toward the hydrant. "You may as well know that somebody is crazy about me, and I have got to stop messing with anybody else like Shirley."

"The Greek girl can be best woman then. Patsy won't mind. All she cares about is marrying me."

Dave studied John Henry's face to see if he was joking; he was not. "You believe that! I'm just sixteen and don't know about girls, but even I know Patsy would throw a hissy you wouldn't believe if anybody else picked the best woman."

"You got to sign the license."

"And she isn't Greek."

"Who?"

"The Greek girl." Dave turned on the water and held his head under the faucet until he thought he felt better. He shook his head, spotting the slicker's fresh khakis. "And nobody nowhere is dumb enough to let me sign no wedding license."

"Everything's worked out. Just trust your uncle J. H. to have the answers," the slicker called back as he headed for his truck wrapped in an aura of ignorance and love.

That afternoon while Dave was not watching Elmo took his door off. The precise time of the removal, as nearly as Dave could determine, was between twelve and one, while he was in the melon vault eating hamburgers and listening to John Henry tell about how he and Patsy might jump off a cliff holding hands if they could not get married.

"We don't have no clifts around here," Dave said.

"Very funny."

"Maybe you could jump off the ice house roof." Still amused, Dave decided to have a peanut pattie for dessert. He went out to the truck to get the morning milk bottle, which he would trade to Mr. Smalley. When he leaned in the driver's side for the bottle he thought the helper's door was ajar at first; after he went around to the other side he was appalled by the unimpeded view through the cab. Absently, he poured out the last drops of chocolate milk. Then he yelled, "He is not going to get away with it."

Dave made a quick and unsuccessful search for the door.

He stalked into the plant, across the brine tanks, and down into the office. Cedric was reared back in Daddy Warbucks' chair reading a *Spicy Detective* magazine. Dave slammed the bottle down on the desk and demanded, "Where is the dirty, atrocity-committin bastard?"

"Which one?"

"Elmo."

"Why, Hotshot, he's gone. He's got them pigs to slop and all. How can I be of help to you?"

Dave pointed a shaking finger at Cedric. "Just don't you never mind, and if you know what's good for you, there will not be any more smartin off." He hurried to the vault, poured out his story, and was dismayed by John Henry's calmness. Actually the slicker seemed to be favorably impressed by Elmo's deed, so Dave blew up and resigned as his best man and daddy. John Henry kept saying, "He didn't really!"and then letting his mouth hang open. Disgusted, Dave returned to the office.

"What are you so steamed up about, Hotshot?"

"I ain't steamed up, Cedric. And you better watch out or I'll give you some of what that hayseed has got coming."

"Well, you sure have been huffing around here with a red face." Cedric cackled; he was always happiest when others were troubled. "Say, did you know me and Vivian went to high school together?"

"Cedric, this is really serious. Not for me, understand. For the company." Dave choked as he tried to put the news in the most devastating form possible.

The manager sobered. He rocked back and forth in the swivel chair while he dog-eared the page he had been reading in the *Spicy Detective*. "The company is grateful."

John Henry appeared in the doorway looking dazed; Dave hated to talk before him since his reaction had been so disappointing, but he could not wait. Dave swallowed. "He took — Elmo took — the door off his side of the truck."

Cedric raised his hands high, slapped the chair arms and laughed so hard he almost fell over backward.

141

Dave's chin trembled. He stared at the ceiling as he re-called that he got the same kind of cooperation everytime he tried to look after Friendly's interests. The company trademark should not be two arms shaking hands; it should be a single fist with the middle finger extended toward an iceman.

Cedric collected himself and wiped his eyes with his sleeve. "And you don't like that?"

"No sir." Dave wished someone would help, but John Henry just stood there looking stupid.

"It was okay to take your door off in spite of the protests of the fine old grey-headed, blue-trousered gentleman who owns this place."

"But Ced, Elmo's just the helper."

Cedric was laughing again, by fits and jerks.

"If people keep taking off parts, pretty soon you don't have no ice truck left," Dave wailed.

"Yeah," John Henry agreed, his face as blank as when he first appeared. "Both doors being off might warp the frame."

Dave caught his breath; he was amazed and thankful. "Yes sir, Ced. By golly, John Henry has gotten the point that I have been trying to make. It could warp my truck something awful and cause Mr. Blackstone to have to spend lots of money on repairs."

The slicker beamed and showed the slight gap between his teeth.

"The big reason for doors on ice trucks is to keep the frame unwarped." Dave used the telephone book to demon-strate the effect of lack of door support. Since Cedric's attitude did not improve, the time came when Dave could no longer stand it. He denounced the manager and led the slicker out to see the ravaged vehicle.

John Henry's face was still without expression. "Elmo sure took her off," he said so many times that Dave finally told him to shut up.

Dave rested his boot on the running board. "Slicker, I'm

as democratic as the next guy — which is what this war is about. But helpers are not icemen. It don't mean I'm better than he is, but the iceman is captain of his ship." He slapped the hood.

The sound brought John Henry around and showed he had not paid attention. "There was a fine article in the *Fortune* magazine on officers and enlisted men and . . . ."

"You know where you can shove *Fortune* magazine," Dave thundered, unwilling to let attention be diverted from the problem, which was the vandalism by a hayseed of Friendly Ice property.

"You want me to help put her back on?"

"No sir. Elmo did this thing by himself; he can fix it by himself," Dave stated. "Besides which, I can't find the door."

John Henry made a sympathetic noise.

Dave said, "He could have at least asked."

"You wouldn't let him."

"Hell no, I wouldn't," Dave practically yelled. "A ice truck, as anybody knows who knows anything at all, has absolutely got to have a minimum of one door or it will warp the frame to a fare-thee-well."

"Well, he sure took her off," John Henry said again.

After Daddy Warbucks got back from lunch Dave grabbed every special that was called in, hoping the old man would see the doorless truck. Usually he carried orders for a hundred pounds or less to the pickup, but he backed up to the dock for twenty-fives. Twice he parked in front of the office and climbed out the helper's side to go into the vault, but the old man said nothing. Near quitting time, Dave became desperate. He backed up to the dock as Daddy Warbucks was tying a twenty-five pounder for two kids to carry on a broomstick.

"Mr. Blackstone," Dave called from the doorless cab.

The old man glanced at Dave with slight interest.

"I was carrying on this argument with myself, and I thought since I couldn't decide that maybe you could tell me so that I could work it out in my mind and be reasonably sure I had reached a correct answer . . . ."

The Friendly proprietor, looking bored, started to leave, and Dave blurted, "Wouldn't it warp a man's frame all to hell if both doors got took off?"

"No more than one door would," Daddy Warbucks said and went into the office to ring up the sale. Dave followed and was starting his phone book demonstration of the warping problem when, with a level gaze, the old man silenced him.

As he took two hundred pounds to the USO, Dave considered quitting Friendly. He could get on at Acme, where they respected their icemen, as was shown by the fact that Ace could be a valued Acme employee while ruining most of the Wake County virgins. Rank had its privileges; and helpers simply were not icemen. One of the main reasons Dave stayed on was that if he quit Elmo would probably get his route and the orange truck, which he would ruin completely.

On the way back to the plant Dave slowed and checked the progress of the scrap drive. The pile was as high as the second story of the courthouse. Some dirty kids played around the edge; those in charge always had to worry about children dragging things out of the heap. Dave turned onto Dyersburg and paused at the Eatwell long enough to honk and wave at Sue. He took a left on Main and found Grandpa's car parked at the lumber yard.

Dave stopped and got out. He sauntered past the office and the long, sweet-smelling stacks of pine and window frames and doors. He heard the click of dominoes and Grandpa's wheezing laugh before he turned the corner. Half a dozen men in work clothes stood and sat around the players. The cuffs of Grandpa's fresh white shirt were turned up and his straw hat was set at a sharp angle. Next to him Dad had his collar open and his tie pulled down. Dr. Millard Edwards, who delivered Ellis, was Grandpa's partner. Dad

144

was playing with Elrod Seitz, the business-getting half of the Morgan-Seitz Plumbing Company.

Dad slammed a domino down and laughed hugely. With a yardstick he moved some pop bottle caps along a wire strung above his head. "That'll cure em of sucking eggs," he said. Dave was always surprised by the way his father talked to people outside the family. He was sad that Dad had never let him or George really know him.

"How are you, boy?" Grandpa clenched a cigar between his teeth as he shuffled the ivory dominoes.

Dad's attitude changed; he had suddenly aged twenty years and wanted Dave to leave so he could be that younger man again. "Are you on your way home?"

"Yes sir. In a little bit." Dave ignored the order that had been put in question form.

Dad flushed.

"That your boy, Malvin?" a spectator asked.

Dad studied his dominoes and mumbled something.

Grandpa said, "He's one of my grandbabies."

Dave laughed with the others; he picked a clean stack of lumber and stretched out with his hands clasped behind his head. Dave knew Dad was fit to be tied, but he could do nothing without looking bad. Dave was sorry about crossing him, but lately he had to set his feet every once in awhile without really understanding why. He worried about Elmo's door until he got tired of it. The smell of sawdust and shavings was nice and he liked the weathered underside of the roof. The clicking of the dominoes, the sliding bottle caps, and the voices were musical and reassuring. Dave was thinking he and George might build and sell houses when someone touched his shoulder and said, "Sorry, young fella."

Dave got up, and some men loaded the lumber on a truck. Suddenly he was very sleepy. "I'll be seeing you," he said. Nobody noticed except Grandpa, whose gold tooth flashed.

Dave took a short cut through high grass and past nail kegs stacked shoulder high. Someone was sitting in a parked car behind the truck; Dave wondered how anyone could stand that heat; then he recognized Hazel. He walked around to the driver's side and bent to speak to her.

"Didn't you see me following you?" she said.

Dave's smile faded. "Nope."

"Don't you ever look in your rear mirror?"

"Sometimes."

"I was back of you all the time. I kept waving." Her forehead and upper lip were damp. "And you left me out here in this hundred and forty heat."

"I didn't see you."

"What were you doing in there?" Her voice had gotten loud and shrill.

"None of your business," he said, flaring up and stalking away, conscious that his heart was beating harder than usual. She started her motor and sped past him. He made no effort to catch her, which was probably what she wanted. New anger surged through him. He was still devising rejoinders when he got back to the plant.

Dave put up his truck and talked to Shy about the frame. Responding to the lack of understanding by the Friendly management he cut a new watermelon and consumed almost a quarter of it. He checked the phone call spike, started home, and was surprised to find Hazel's car parked in front of the laundry. He walked faster as he passed her. She came down on the horn; he gave her a hard look and considered going on, but she would raise some more rumpus and all the laundry women would see it. He put his head in the window. Her mascara was smeared, and she dabbed at her forehead with a wad of Kleenex. "Get in," she ordered.

Dave opened the door, decided he would drive, and went around to her side. She moved over reluctantly. He drove two blocks and stopped in front of the wagon yard.

"How come we're stopping?"

"Because I live a block that way, And because I don't have to take your guff."

She compressed her lips and stared straight ahead. When he took the door handle she said, "Wait a minute."

"Why?" Heat from the red brick pavement seemed to come right through the floorboard; the patching asphalt had melted enough to run.

"Just wait."

He shoved down the handle and the door lock released.

"I won't anymore."

He sighed and opened the door. "Won't what?"

She grabbed his arm and tried to reach past to shut the door. "Give you anymore guff. Let's talk."

"It won't do any good."

"Let's do, anyhow."

"Have you got enough gas?"

She nodded.

Dave started the car, shifted gears, and headed north on Kentuckytown, vowing to turn back if Hazel said one wrong thing. They passed a city limits sign riddled by generations of dove hunters. She scooted over and took his hand.

At McGrew's First and Last Chance Grocery, Dave parked under the huge oak and bought Pepsi-Colas. Hazel sat in the shade on the bench usually occupied by loafers. Ordinarily kids would be swinging in the old tire that dangled from a cable. It was the coolest spot around, but nobody was willing to come through the heat to reach it today. Hazel, wilted and worried and mixed up, was not as pretty as she had been.

"That breeze feels good," Dave said to cheer her up.

"But I wanted you to take me away from everything."

Dave shoved the tire swing. "You haven't done anything lately but complain."

"I got my reasons."

He caught the tire and gave it another push. "You don't have any problem that ain't homemade."

Her eyes narrowed. "You've changed for the bad, and

147

I know why. You got somebody else and don't care a hoot for me."

He wanted to put his arms around her, but that would only make matters worse. "I care a whole lot about you, Hazel." He stopped the tire and hooked an arm around the cable. She looked as if she were going to come after him, so he added, "but what could we have? So we got to knock it off and don't see one another again."

She held the brown Pepsi bottle before her and ran a thumbnail along the edge of the soggy paper label.

"You see?"

She put the bottle down on the bench. "I see that you are so wrapped up in that tacky blonde that people that love you can't even talk to you." She flounced over to the car and Dave followed.

"I don't care two cents about her. Move over."

"Shirley," she crowed "is her name. Just try to say it's not."

"You're nuts." Dave saw McGrew standing in the doorway; no telling how long he had been there. All the way to town Hazel went on about Shirley. Dave was grateful that she accused him of things he could truthfully deny. "Hazel, this arguing just goes to prove that we got to let one another alone."

"How come you didn't leave me any ice this morning?"

"Your card wasn't up."

"It was, too. I put it up, and later on I checked. And when I come looking for you it was still up."

"Don't you see how bad things have got?" Dave wagged his head sorrowfully. Nothing else was said until he stopped a block from home.

"I bet you took that blond-headed Shirley bitch some ice."

Dave was horrified. He had never heard a woman use such language. Men and boys swore but not beautiful women; he was repelled and, at the same time, drawn to her more than ever. She was his love and was lost and

148

beyond saving. "You orter be ashamed," he said as he got out of the car and stalked off. He did not answer when she called his name nor did he give any sign that he noticed when she hit the horn. And though it sounded as if she ground off every single gear tooth, he ignored her as the car shot past him.

It was partly a dream, but mostly not. Dave was at the bottom of a darkness so thick he had trouble breathing. Then he knew he was lying on the floor and the sound that came through was Ellis' crying.

"Aw my," Dave said as he sat up and tried to understand what was happening. He got to his feet holding the sofa cushion. Ellis was standing by him squawling. "What's wrong?"

The little brother ground his fists in his eyes and kept howling.

"What in the world is wrong?" Dave started to replace the sofa cushion when he saw the bleeding cut on Ellis' big toe. In a single movement he picked up Ellis and started for the bathroom. He sat the little brother on the side of the tub. "Don't look at your foot," he ordered, and as Ellis was about to disobey, "unless you want to get sick and upchuck."

It occurred to Dave that blood would ruin the rug; he told Ellis to be still and ran to the living room to squeeze water on the spots. When he returned, Ellis was staring at the bloody foot and was very pale.

"Here, let's get you so you don't fall over." Dave had Ellis lie down on the bath mat. He wiped away the blood and found the long, deep gash. "What in the heck were you doing?"

Ellis would not stop weeping long enough to answer. When Dave took medicine and bandages from behind the mirror, Ellis raised his head and blubbered something

149

about the medicine stinging. Dave was getting tired of Ellis' howling and jerking his foot away. "It's just alcohol and monkey blood."

Ellis increased his volume at the mention of alcohol. Dave stuck his finger in the little brother's face and said, "You be still or you'll really have something to cry about."

Ellis whimpered and looked pitiful.

"What happened anyhow, Buddy Boy?" Dave set about making repairs. Ellis tried to answer, but all Dave understood was that a butcher knife was involved. "Okay. Don't rub your eyes. You'll have them all sore."

There was a movement in the hall; Dave hoped it was Mother home from her meeting, but it was only Reedy and Otho and T. A. acting innocent. They had scattered when whatever happened took place, and then curiosity had gotten the better of them. "Hello, Mr. Totten," Otho said.

Dave addressed the tallest one. "What happened, Reedy?"

Ellis cut his volume, probably to hear better.

"I told him not to get that knife. Didn't I, Otho? But he wouldn't listen. Would he, Otho?"

Dave sighed. "I know you did all you could, Reedy."

"We did too," Otho said, "me and T. A. tried to keep it from happening."

"They did not either," Ellis yelled.

"You're all in the clear." Dave sat back on his haunches, deciding how the bandage should go.

Reedy, confident now, began a long, disjointed story.

"Are you through, David?" Ellis sniffed and tried to see.

"Be still. T. A., get me the scissors out of the sewing machine." He pointed. "In that back corner room."

Reedy continued his narrative with appropriate gestures.

"Otho, has my mother been home since I been asleep?"

"I don't know, Mr. Totten."

"She come in and then went grocery buyin," Reedy volunteered.

150

T. A. ran in holding the scissors in front of him; Dave berated him for his carelessness.

"Are you a doctor, Mr. Totten?"

"Otho, I told you I'm just sixteen."

Dinty waddled into the bathroom and flopped down on the white tile beside Ellis.

Reedy got louder as he lost their attention, which grated on Dave's nerves and he told Reedy to shut up.

After awhile Reedy asked, "Can Ellis come out and play?"

Dave sighed. "No, Reedy, only a few minutes ago he damn near cut his foot off and he's still peaked. He better stay quiet until Mother gets here."

"Yeah, maybe he can come out then, Mr. Totten," Otho said.

T. A. handed Ellis a toy rifle. "Here's your gun."

"Can Dinty come out then?" Reedy asked.

Dave was tired of them. "If he wants to. If he doesn't want to, no, he can't come outside."

Reedy called him, but the old dog did not move. When Reedy picked up Dinty's forelegs and tried to walk him, Dave snapped. "No, dammit. Get out, all of you."

The three friends backed into the hall and said their good-byes. As they went out Dave heard Reedy say, "I never seen anybody lay down to get their toe bandaged." Then the screen door slammed.

Dave put up the bandages and medicine. "Can you make it upstairs?"

Ellis, using the rifle as a cane, tried walking on his heel but did not do well. Dave carried him upstairs. "Let's lay you down awhile."

Dinty's toenails rattled on the stairs as he followed Dave.

"I want to be on George's bed, David." Ellis pointed with the rifle and they turned into George's room. Ellis stood on one foot, balancing against the chest, while Dave turned down the bedspread. Dave strained to open the window; the paint had not been mixed properly and every

151

sash in the house stuck. Finally the window broke loose. A piece of the antenna from George's old crystal radio was still held in place by the screen.

Ellis lay holding his rifle. One hand dangled off the bed touching Dinty, who had collapsed on the rug. Dave sat in the chair that always seemed so small with George in it; now it no longer accommodated him. "You tell me if you get sick. And say so quick enough that I can do something about it. You hear?"

"Uh huh."

"What happened? I couldn't follow Reedy."

"He didn't tell me not to do anything," Ellis began.

"Yeah, but what happened?"

"Zorro, he was on at the Lyric yesterday, and I got down there and the cold thing wouldn't work, so I didn't go. And Reedy was Cisco, and I was Zorro, and when I threw the knife down, it cut my foot."

Dave wished he had listened to Reedy, but then he decided he really did not need to know the whole story. "The air conditioner went out at the Lyric again?"

"Uh huh."

"Did they give back your money?"

"We never got in." Ellis held the rifle up and studied it.

Dave hung his leg over the chair arm the way George did. The room was musty. On the chest was George's boxing trophy; his certificate for making All State in football hung on the wall. The boxer statuette seemed smaller than it used to, and the paper in the black frame was turning yellow.

"When will George come home?" Ellis put the gun down and yawned.

"Pretty soon."

"After the war?"

"Yes."

"I can sleep in his bed sometimes." Ellis shut his eyes and his voice trailed off.

"Do you really remember George?"

152

Ellis waited for a long time and answered from the edge of sleep, "I remember."

Earlier, Sue had mentioned that she had a surprise for him, but he was unprepared for anything so fine. He took the wheel of the 1940 Pontiac and said, "How come he let us have it?"

Sue leaned her head against his shoulder. "He does nice things sometimes, for no reason."

Dave fought the impulse to double-clutch as he pulled away from the curb. "She sure handles nice. Where to?"

"Anywhere. But we stand a better chance of using it again if we come in early."

Dave put his arm around her and weighed the options. They could go court up a storm and maybe not get the Pontiac as often or they could spend a little while together and perhaps become regular users. Dave set out for the Dutch Inn, hoping for many evenings in Sarge's car. "I had a bad time today. Elmo took his door off, and I don't think Daddy Warbucks is going to make him put it back on."

"Can't you?"

"Can't I what?"

"Make him put it back on?"

"Naturally. I am the captain of that truck, and if Mr. Blackstone hadn't acted like he did I would have made Elmo put it back on. But the old man showed his true colors. I will not kill myself protecting the rolling stock when he don't care."

Sue did not really understand the problem. "I wish they would do right," she said. She began singing along with the radio in a soft voice, whispering the best lines to Dave.

He stopped across from the Dutch Inn and waited for the traffic to clear.

"Can we get curb service? I don't look like going in."

That was for the best. Dave did not want to expose her to the general run of his friends yet. He parked on the north lot, and a heavy, thirtyish blonde hurried out to the car. Her black slacks were tight enough across the rear to ride up and pucker just below the cowboy belt supporting her moneychanger.

"Hi Virgie." Dave wanted Sue to think he knew everyone in town. He ordered while Virgie inspected Sue.

"John Henry Panky is over there." She walked away resting an empty tray on her hip.

Dave did not look, for fear that Shirley was there, too, but within minutes John Henry was at Sarge's car. Dave was dismayed, but good manners made him hide his feelings. He narrowed his eyes and asked testily, "Anybody with you?"

"Just only Patsy. I got to talk to you." He climbed into the back seat without being invited.

"This is John Henry," Dave told Sue.

"I know. He buys hot chocolate from us." She turned sideways in the seat. "Why don't you bring your date over?"

"Oh hell no," Dave blurted out, then tried to put a better face on his statement. "She is probably tired."

Anxious to divert Sue's attention he said, "How do you like the car, Slicker?"

John Henry said to Sue, "No thanks. I got to take her home."

Patsy was sitting in John Henry's car wearing her usual scowl. Dave said, "Well, I hate that you got to take her home."

"Look here." John Henry handed Dave a small jewelry box. "They are rings."

"Yeah." Dave passed them to Sue, who made the usual fuss.

"One is hers, and the other is mine."

"I thought the big one was for her ankle." Dave chuckled, pleased with himself.

154

Sue glowered. "That was mean."

John Henry paid no attention to Dave. "I got it all figured out how we're gonna do it."

"Him and Patsy thinks they are going to get married," Dave told Sue.

"We'll drive up to Ardmore and me and Patsy will go in the courthouse. She can show her birth certificate, since she's old enough, and I'll claim my daddy is sick, and I have to take the consent thing to him. So we come out and drive around awhile, and you sign it, and we waste some more time. Then me and Patsy go back and get the license."

Dave studied the sincerity and stupidity in John Henry's face. "They ain't gonna go for that."

"I'm older than you, David, and I have had lots of experience."

Sue handed back the rings and said, "They're lovely. When will you get married?"

"Right quick." John Henry, with some effort, looked away from Sue. "She sure is pretty, Dave. My cousin married a Greek."

Dave groaned. "I told you five times that she's not Greek." Nobody ever listened to him.

"Dave, that chewing tobacco sure is boogerin up your teeth."

"Tobacco!" Sue echoed. "That's why you taste so funny."

"He's joking." Dave wished John Henry would go away. Patsy kept peering at them from behind a magazine that she held too high to be reading, trying for a good look so she could describe Sue to Shirley. Suddenly Dave found himself looking Patsy square in the eye; she turned away quickly and honked for John Henry to return.

Honking was the signal for curb service, so Virgie responded. Patsy, becoming more embarrassed and angry, waved Virgie off; her mouth formed several words Dave was slow about using, even in football practice. He shuddered. Patsy would hide John Henry and probably neither

155

of them would realize that what she was really angry about was not getting a good look at Sue.

"You are gonna do it?" John Henry asked.

"I said I would and I will try to get you married."

John Henry let out a whoop and smiled at the dour Patsy. "We ought to cut some watermelons to celebrate."

Dave glared; the idiot knew better than to bring Patsy and Sue together.

"Yes. Please, let's do," Sue said.

Dave was aware of a conscience gone bad; keeping her from his friends had hurt her. "He was kidding, Sue. Besides I cut one this afternoon." He squeezed her shoulder, but there was no response.

"Yeah, I was kidding. You shouldn't cut them things so late. It'll be slick tomorrow." Patsy sat down hard on John Henry's horn, and he said his goodbyes in a hurry as Virgie came out with a tray on her hip. She thrust her head forward, glowered at Patsy, and as her lips moved Dave recognized some of the words Patsy had just used. He was appalled; women were supposed to be nicer than men.

"It will be fun to go along when they get married." Sue was making an effort to overcome her disappointment.

"It won't be much."

"I bet you never have been to a wedding."

"No. And I probably won't go to this one. He don't know what he's talking about."

Sue's shoulders drooped and she studied her hands.

When Virgie came to get the tray she said. "That Patsy is going to get her hair pulled out one of these days."

"She sure does need it." Patsy and John Henry were yelling at each other when Dave drove past. They cruised around while Dave tried, with slight success, to raise Sue's spirits. He took her home early, hoping to impress Sergeant Wales. When there were no lights burning Dave felt betrayed; no one would witness his sacrifice, no one would see him bringing the sergeant's car and daughter home at a ridiculous hour. He considered taking Sue parking, but decided that would anger her. As they went in, Dave slammed the front door and walked heavy.

"Be quiet," Sue whispered as he deliberately ran into the coffee table and made its legs scrape. She turned on the table lamp next to the divan.

"In the morning, be sure and tell your Dad when we came in."

"I certainly will," she stated. She was peevish; Dave knew he had better watch his step. He switched off the light and they sat in the darkness listening to the radio. The ten o'clock news told about the contest between Bricker and Dewey for the Republican presidential nomination. Dave broke off a kiss, and said, "Hey, be sure you say we were here before the news."

She jerked loose and moved out of reach. "Yes, David. I will do everything in my power to make sure you get to use my father's car again."

"It isn't that," Dave said.

"What is it?"

"Well, I don't know, but it isn't that."

"What you are, David, is plain old selfish."

They sat in silence at opposite ends of the sofa for a long time. Dave coughed every once in awhile and hummed along with a couple of songs, determined that she speak first. But she was too stubborn to do the right thing; it fell to him to be the peacemaker. She did not resist as he brought her back to lie with her head in his lap. As the radio began playing "My Ideal," Sue touched his face and said, "I love you," and he kissed her so she would not notice his failure to answer. Later they decided to go to the movies Saturday if the air conditioning was fixed.

"I better get home," he said.

"Yes. I have to be downtown early."

"Yeah, well, it's about that time."

"It's been hard to get up lately."

"Well, I better be on my way."

Sue opened the door, and they went through the whole

157

routine again until they both were self-conscious about the delay. He moved out onto the porch; she started to close the door.

"Sue."

"Yes?"

"Tell your father I appreciated his generosity when you say how early we got in."

She slammed the door so hard that Dave was afraid she had disturbed Sergeant Wales.

10

All day Tuesday the tension remained between Dave and Elmo. Wind whipped clear through the cab while the helper perched on the huge pillow that had been a forty-eight pound flour sack. Occasionally Elmo spat into the Folger's coffee can; his expression reminded Dave of an eastern ruler sitting on scales to receive his weight in jewels.

Twice Elmo put his foot on the running board, which was sickening. Dave, hurt and resentful, kept both legs inside the truck. He flinched as Cedric smirked whenever he saw the truck; more painful was Daddy Warbucks' callousness about the warping of his rolling stock as he noticed, without comment, the lack of door support. Worst of all, Dave feared his employer might use the situation to get both doors put back on the truck.

Dave treated the helper with his usual courtesy, but he intended to leave no doubt about the seriousness of the door removal. Elmo was reserved, too; in fact, he was aloof to an uppity degree.

At the close of the day, Dave sat in the Friendly office staring at the red and black symbols on the Black Draught calendar. He was dispirited. There was no hope of saving the truck. He was going to donate Hazel to John Henry. He had to find out how the Lyric's air conditioning repairs were coming. But nothing seemed really important. He had not even had a last look at the scrap pile, which would be hauled off tomorrow. Someone had drawn a moustache and glasses on the naked calendar girl at Sadler's Grocery, which would have torn him up normally; now that atrocity was only another minor nuisance. It was all he could do to put one foot in front of the other.

Of all the Friendly people, John Henry had behaved best. He remained completely sober whenever the door was mentioned, perhaps in awe of Elmo's daring, but to his eternal credit, John Henry was the first to appreciate the warping problem.

That night Sue pestered him to know what was wrong, but he refused to bother her with problems beyond her powers. Sergeant Wales was still up. Dave spent two hours looking at photographs of Sue's friends and relatives. Dave said he enjoyed seeing them, but the people looked like all the sense had been bred out of them. By the time her parents went to bed, Sue was tired; they only courted thirty minutes, and Dave left hacked. On the way home Dave ate a dozen doughnuts and got sick. He stepped in Dinty's water pan — Ellis had left it on the back porch — and got water in his shoe. When he slept he dreamed that George took Dinty up in a bomber and people said George had crashed.

Wednesday started out no better; the milk bottle slipped out of Dave's hands and broke. His stomach growled as he stared at the brown mess on the doctor's sidewalk. He threw the broken glass down the storm sewer and wondered how he could make it through the morning.

Elmo was already at the plant when Dave got there. In his lap was the *Spicy Range* magazine he had left in the truck yesterday. Dave had thrown it away, but evidently Elmo had dug it out of the trash. They exchanged sullen greetings.

After the first load Daddy Warbucks leaned in Elmo's side and complimented him on doing a good job, which made Elmo even more disagreeable. Somewhere between the cotton compress and roundhouse the helper decided he owned the glove compartment since it was on his side of the truck.

"You are kidding," Dave said.

"You figure that?" The helper sneered as he dumped the glove compartment contents on Dave's half of the seat. Elmo picked up something from the pile, studied it, and spat loudly into his coffee can. When Dave realized Elmo had old Shirley's picture, he snatched it away, filled with indignation; for all Elmo knew, Shirley might be his wife. Dave would have beaten hell out of Elmo if he were younger and not so dried up. "That was a rotten thing."

Elmo stuck out his chin, smoothed the *Spicy Range*, and laid it in the glove compartment. After Dave let him off for breakfast he considered not going back for him. He went down to the square, sat on his fender, ate doughnuts, drank milk, and watched the scrap hauled away.

On the courthouse steps Levi Hackley and a two-piece hillbilly band were promoting last minute scrap donations. Levi hugged the microphone and did an impersonation of Sonny Tufts. Dave was thinking that Levi made him ill when he remembered he had sworn off doughnuts last night; he made an exception for the last two since it was bad to waste food.

Levi made a remark he thought was humorous and Dave sighed. Levi was the high school band drum major until two years ago. The slogan on the banner draped across the courthouse, "Give your scrap and slap a Jap," had been written by Levi, who gazed at it from time to time.

The public address system squealed as Levi said, "And now, Miss Ella Fears is giving those famous hitching posts from the Fears' mansion." The crowd clapped politely, and Dave wanted to punch Levi's face. Miss Ella's house was no mansion, and she and Levi knew it; it was an old five-room place with the kitchen water and drain pipes˜outside on the back wall.

"Yes, yes," Levi said to be sure everyone recognized

him as the popular host of the One O Five Club. "Miss Ella, won't you please say a few words?"

Miss Ella would not talk into the microphone so no one ever knew what she was saying. Four colored fellows were pushing a Model T — minus tires and motor — up to the pile. Carl Morris, the jeweler, contributed two tiny dumbbells; it was little wonder that Carl was built like a sack of dough.

Dave was miserable. A skinny old lady was talking past the P. A. system, some Negroes had sacrificed a car, Mr. Morris had no workout equipment, and Dave was queasy on doughnuts again and wanting to cry over his uselessness; he had to give something. He forced the last doughnut and ran across to Monkey Wards' warehouse. With the wrenches and screwdrivers J. C. Overshine lent him he soon had the bumpers off the truck. He found himself walking, as if in a dream, toward the scrap pile.

Levi's voice boomed out, "Here is young David Totten carrying . . . . What are those, David?"

"Bumpers." Dave wished he had left them last night.

"Come up and say a few words."

Dave knew that was a device to get rid of Miss Ella; she had remained at the microphone after she finished whatever it was she said.

"Thank you, Miss Ella," Levi said, for the eighth time.

"You're welcome," she repeated and did not move.

Levi frowned at her. "Young David Totten is giving some bumpers." A wind gust blew the Slap-the-Jap banner against the courthouse. Levi glanced up, fearfully.

Dave dropped the bumpers and went back to the truck.

Levi thanked Miss Ella again and, as if rebuking her, said, "Master Totten, young Totten, prefers to stay out of the limelight. Brother to one of Wake County's greatest heroes. A modest young man. But Lawton will not forget what he did here today. Yes, yes."

The band broke into something between "Praise the Lord and Pass the Ammunition" and "The Old Grey Mare."

Dave lowered his head, promising to whip Levi at the first opportunity.

As Dave drove away, the engine ran better than before. He cut the wheels this way and that; she even handled easier. He reveled in the benefits, which were, of course, not the main reason for his generosity; the bumpers might be melted into bullets that would save George from a clutch of Messerschmitts. Dave was seized by a great good will toward everyone, even Levi, although he was a draft-dodger, probably. At Jiggs' place, Elmo got in without noticing the bumper loss; his show of suspicion was because Dave had almost forgiven him and it showed.

It was nearly quitting time when Daddy Warbucks learned about the bumpers. Dave had gone by the office to demonstrate that he held no grudges about Elmo's door, and Mr. Blackstone began a sermon on the complete wearing out of clothing. Dave was feeling the faded blue trousers again when the telephone rang.

A premonition made Dave shiver, and his blood froze as the old man said into the mouthpiece, "Yes, Miss Ella."

Dave discovered a message from Hazel on the phone spike. He moved toward the door pretending to read it. Mr. Blackstone snapped his fingers and motioned for him to stay. Dave swallowed hard. The old man's eyes were as clear and lightly blue as a piece of ice newly pulled from the tanks.

"Yes, Miss Ella, we are proud we could contribute. Yes, we have to, for our soldier boys. Yes, I'll miss those hitching posts. They were the last in town. Yes ma'am, it is good to get you back as a customer. A man will be out first thing tomorrow." Between answers he glared at Dave, with his mouth compressed like a rabbit's.

When he hung up Dave said, "Uh, we got a new customer, huh? I bet we are going to get lots more."

The old man stood up tiredly. "You wait here." He disappeared across the tanks.

Dave stared, without seeing, at Hazel's note. He wished

163

old ladies would mind their own business long enough for people to break their own surprises. Daddy Warbucks was back almost immediately, his face a deep red.

"I bet we could wind up with a good half of Acme's customers because of the way we are supporting the war effort."

"I want my bumpers back, Totten."

"You mean you don't want to give them?" It did not sound as strong as he intended, so Dave added, "To the support of our troops?"

"I want those bumpers."

"You didn't get mad when Elmo took his door off."

"Well, by God, I'm mad now."

"I never heard of no truck gettin warped over a bumper donation to help win a war." Dave started to add that he was surprised to hear Mr. Blackstone's swearing but thought better of it.

The old man stood in the center of the room looking as if he were about to set up like a batch of concrete.

Dave stayed out of reach. "I don't know if I can get them."

"I want my bumpers, Totten."

Dave marveled at the range of meaning the old man could get into such a simple statement. "What could we say to Miss Ella and those who were so happy over our donation?"

"Our donation! They are *my* bumpers off *my* truck." Mr. Blackstone spread his arms. Dave would not have been a bit surprised if the old man had hit him. He started to the truck but turned back when he saw Cedric and John Henry and Shy inspecting it. He flopped down in the far corner of the melon vault. John Henry came in and they chunked ice picks into the old, water-soaked wood.

"What are you going to do, Dave?"

"I don't know."

"They need carpenter's helpers at the camp again."

The door opened and Cedric stood there listening to

someone. Finally he came in, his shoulders hunched and his face grim. "Damn, Hotshot."

Dave dropped his eyes.

"I get more pure dee hell on account of you than the whole rest of this business. How come you did it?"

"I don't know."

Cedric sighed. "Mr. Blackstone called your dad. You are supposed to go, right now, and get the bumpers and report to your father's office."

Dave thought he might level with Cedric on what kind of a sorry kid Warren was, but he was caught too solidly. Besides Warren was all right except for being stupid and a smart aleck.

"I would go quick, was I you." Cedric's tone changed. "Without bumpers if you even touch anything you will ruin the grille."

The injustice of it all suddenly flared up within Dave's breast. "If that sawed-off hillbilly son-of-a-bitch hadn't of took his door off . . . ."

Cedric left before Dave finished. Dave glared at John Henry, spoiling for a fight, and threw his ice pick at the watermelons. John Henry pulled the pick, smoothed the hole, and turned the unmarked side out. There was real compassion in his voice as he said, "I'm sorry, Dave."

By the time Dave got to the square, most of the scrap was gone. The area where he had left the bumpers had been cleared. Levi and the hillbilly band had departed. There remained only some whittlers, the crane operator, and a truck driver, who hunkered beneath a tree studying a *Sheena, Queen of the Jungle* comic book. Dave climbed the ladder on the side of the crane; the operator, wearing a dirty blue baseball cap and a T-shirt, seemed surprised.

"You remember me?" Dave yelled over the engine noise.

The crane operator's eyes narrowed as if he read lips. "Yeah."

"I don't guess those bumpers are still around?"

The man grinned evilly. He had several teeth missing.

165

"You wasn't supposed to give them, I bet."

"I damn sure was," Dave lied. He jumped down, boiling; even complete strangers gave him sass. He circled the remnants of the scrap heap, carefully avoiding the crane. He was about to decide that there were no bumpers when something bright caught his eye. He climbed up on a truck motor block for a closer look but found only a strip of chrome from a soda fountain.

He was almost to the truck when the crane operator cut his motor, yelled, "Did you find them bumpers?" and laughed cruelly.

Dave could think of no appropriate reply; good answers were always hard to come by. The truck did look awfully naked. Probably its appearance would be improved by taking off the bumper mounts, and Dave pondered donating them. But he could think of no one — with the possible exception of Grandpa — who would not fault him for it. He cruised past Dad's office several times before going in. He stopped at the secretary's desk and said, "Dad isn't here, is he, Mrs. Gillory?"

"Yes, he is, but you are to take a seat and wait."

"Is he real mad?"

Mrs. Gillory had taught school before she married. "One does not get mad. One goes mad. One gets angry."

Dave said he had wondered about that and thanked her. He leafed through an insurance magazine. It would be nice not to have problems, like Mrs. Gillory, the crane operator, and all those who made life hard on others. The mark of someone with troubles was his concern for the feelings of everyone else.

Dad's door opened, but Dave kept reading the magazine until his name was called. He went in, sat down, rolled up the magazine, and groped for conversation. "They are doing some painting over at Monkey Wards," he said, wishing Dad would not stand over him.

"Did you get back the bumpers?" Dad's voice trembled.

"Oh, yeah, I was going to tell you about that." He tilted

the chair backward to see his father's face. "They already hauled them away."

Dad hurried around the desk as if he were afraid of what he might do. "Don't get smart with me. You sassed Mr. Blackstone."

"But, Dad, I . . . ."

"And sit straight." His eyebrows came close together and his mouth twitched.

"Yes sir."

"You are going to make this thing right."

Dave rolled the magazine tighter. "Yes sir."

Dad turned to the window, his hands clasped behind him. Everytime Dave saw him he looked thinner. "You knew that was wrong?"

Dave's eyes went moist. "I don't know why I did it."

His father whirled about. "You must know. We are worried sick about George, and you stay out to all hours. And now you give away something that isn't yours." His hands trembled and he seemed very old.

Dave said, "I'll get her taken care of." In the reception room he slapped the magazine against his leg to show Mrs. Gillory that he had not been scared. He pitched the magazine onto the couch; whoever tried to read it would have a terrible time keeping it flat.

Dave called the Ford house and searched three junk yards before admitting that he was not going to find any bumpers. Everybody said there was a war on, which was what got him into the mess in the first place. He wondered whether John Henry could sign as his father for him to join the Marines. The courthouse clock sounded three o'clock; it seemed much later. He saw Sue behind the register at the Eatwell; he could stop and talk to her, but Theo would be nosing around. Dave parked at the depot and sat in the truck for awhile before he went in to the phone booth and gave Central the number. When Hazel answered, he said, "Can I come talk to you?"

Hazel was breathing hard into the mouthpiece; at least

Dave hoped it was her and not the operator listening in. "Huh," he said. She was probably considering whether she could make some points off him first. She did not press her luck. She said, "I guess."

Although the yards were empty along Pendleton, Dave felt as if the whole world watched him as he pulled into Hazel's driveway. He took his hooks, which put a better face on things, as he went in. Hazel was waiting just inside the front door, wearing yellow shorts and thick-soled sandals. She threw her arms around him, increasing his uneasiness. "Ted, he's not here?" Dave said.

She pulled his head down and kissed him. "I am so glad you're here. I missed you so much."

"Yeah, me too," Dave said, looking around to be sure Ted was not lying in wait with a shotgun. John Henry had told him about a *True Detective* story where a good-looking wife would lure a man into her apartment and the husband would shoot him for his money. "But I have got to talk to you."

She led him into her room and they sat down on the side of the bed. While Dave was deciding what it was that he wanted to say, she pulled him down on top of her. He wished Sue knew as much about kissing as Hazel did. After awhile he lay back, agitated and breathing hard.

Dave wanted to tell her the bumper story but realized she could be of no help even if she were interested, which she would not be. He stared at the checked design in the ceiling paper, then stopped for fear he would hypnotize himself and be completely defenseless. Her head was on his shoulder, and she moved her hand across his chest.

"Hey, how did you get that new ice card?"

"Ted went for it the day I tore up the old one."

Dave laughed, problem-free for the first time since the donation. He kissed her again and forgot everything else. Before he knew it her blouse was open to the waist, her shorts and panties were hanging from an ankle, and she was tugging at the sweaty, red-striped, T-shirt.

168

Dave raised up on an elbow. Her mouth was wider and her lips thicker than he remembered, and she had a hardness he had not noticed before. He pulled the shirt down.

"What is wrong?" she demanded. "That's the third time you backed away."

Dave shook his head. "I just don't know, Hazel."

"Maybe it is that little, silly, blond-headed thing you are so crazy about."

"I don't give a hoot for her. And I sure as hell didn't come here to get fought with."

"Why did you come? That's what I'd like to know."

He had no answer.

"Tell me," she insisted.

"I don't know."

"One thing is for sure; you don't want me." She bounced off the bed, kicking the panties across the room. She went to the dresser and took a pack of Camels out of her purse. Dave sat on the side of bed, trying not to look at her bare rear as she lighted the cigarette.

She turned, pulling the blouse shut; it ended just below the navel. Her hips flared the way they should and her legs were long and perfectly formed, according to the calendars, Sears' catalogues, and Rita Hayworth movies Dave had seen. She blew smoke toward the ceiling as she stood before him. He looked past her to the photograph of Clark Gable in his Air Corps uniform; Dave had never known anyone to buy a Kresses frame for the movie star picture that came in it.

"You never have seen a woman naked?" Hazel moved into his line of vision.

"Quite a few," he said.

Suddenly she changed again. She knelt before him, and her face was soft. "Don't you know what I feel about you?"

"Me, too, Hazel."

"Don't you want me, David?"

"Well yeah, but . . . ." She was at the T-shirt again; he pulled it down. "But I got these troubles, Hazel."

169

"You're afraid," she charged.

"Hell no." He forced a laugh. "But I actually came to talk about my bumpers."

"Bumpers!" Her voice got shrill and loud. "You're nothing but a damn kid."

He reached for her, but she dodged and retreated as she puffed the cigarette and poured abuse on him. "A damn dumb ice-hauling kid," she yelled. "Get out."

Dave was going to tell her he did not have to take that kind of guff, but she ran into the bathroom and locked the door. He could hear her bawling for awhile, and he thought up a bunch of things to say when she came out, but then she got quiet and would not answer when he shouted through the door. She was just contrary enough to write a note about him and then kill herself. He took his ice hooks and peered out the front door. Mrs. Ethel Butcher was digging her flower bed; he waited until her back was turned and sprinted for the truck, wondering if Mrs. Butcher could have heard Hazel.

By the time Dave got to the lumber yard his breathing was normal again, and his excitement had become a headache and a steady groin pain. He drove past the shingles and ship lap and stopped at the heavy stuff. Tooter Boswell measured the bumper mounts, advised on bolts and washers, and sawed a couple of pieces from the two-by-twelve stock. He asked, "How come you walkin around like that?"

"Got the rocks," Dave said.

Tooter broke into a toothless grin and said, "You young fellers."

Dave held the two-by-twelves as Tooter marked where the holes would go. Tooter drilled the planks and they bolted them onto the bumper mounts. Tooter stepped back to admire the wooden bumpers. "Doggies, they look good."

Dave had hoped the planks would blend into the truck's appearance, so they would not seem so large. He was terribly disappointed and worried. As he paid Tooter he was

170

certain that he should have used two-by-eights, even though they would have given the grille less protection. Tooter planed off the ends of the bumpers. He insisted upon showing them to the domino players, but while he was gone after them, Dave drove away. He got inside the plant without attracting attention and found Cedric in the office.

"How was Mr. Blackstone?" Dave asked.

"Still upset."

"Well, I got it taken care of."

Cedric's mouth dropped open, costing him the frazzled matchstick he had been chewing. "I didn't think you could do it, Hotshot."

"Well, I did."

"Where's the truck?"

"Out back."

Cedric got a look at the truck while they were still in the machinery room and was convulsed with laughter. He staggered to the truck and fell across the fender roaring and slobbering.

Dave was miserable.

"Oh me, Hotshot," Cedric would say as he was about to straighten up, then collapse again.

"I wouldn't laugh if your ass was in a sling." Dave was bursting with indignation. "I may paint the bumpers silver to make them even more natural."

That set Cedric off again. When finally he composed himself he said, "How come you're hobbling around?"

"Don't you never mind, Cedric, but if you ever do anything worthwhile I am not going to do one thing but laugh."

Cedric brought O. P. and everyone else in the world out for a look. Dave could hear them clear out to the street as he started home.

Ellis and Otho were down on the ground in front of the tree house. Dave stood behind them a few minutes before they noticed him.

"Hi, Mr. Totten," Otho said.

"David, how do you get a doodlebug out?"

"Yeah, Mr. Totten, how do you?"

"Listen, Otho, I'm not but sixteen. I don't even have a driver's license."

"But how, David?" Ellis had a purple shadow all around his mouth from drinking Poly Pop. The clean bandage Mother had put on his foot last night was loose and dirty. Burnt matchsticks were scattered on the bare earth around the doodlebug hole.

"You lean close and say 'Doodlebug, doodlebug, your house is on fire.' "

"We done that, Mr. Totten, but nobody came out."

"Listen Otho, you think you can remember not to call me Mister if I kick your butt everytime you do it?"

"Uh huh, Mr. Totten," Otho said.

Dave sighed.

"It's how you talk to doodlebugs that matters."

Ellis looked up at him. "David, did you ever see a doodlebug?"

"Lots of them."

"What did they look like?"

"Like doodlebugs."

On the way in Dave stopped to pet Dinty, who stumbled to his feet, panting. He cut his eyes, so that a patch of black showed in the corners, and pushed against Dave's hand. "You miss George, don't you old fella?" Dave thought it was nice to sit in the shade with someone who was so glad to see him.

Mother called to him out the back door, "David, you're late."

"Yes ma'am, I had a bad day." He hugged her as he came in. "Did we hear from George?"

"Not today." She touched the stretched front of his T-shirt. "How do you get these so out of shape?"

He smoothed the shirt. "Oh, just working. Delivering ice

172

bags your shirts on you." Dave got away from her in a hurry. He tried to take a nap, but Hazel kept calling him a kid. And there were her hips and legs and all the things he should have said. He could not get his mind off what happened, but he was relieved about her.

After giving up on the nap he found a pencil and paper and sprawled across the bed to write George. The *Ladies Home Journal* said it was bad to worry overseas servicemen, so Dave kept his troubles to himself. He wrote about how Mary liked Sue. He told George how much he weighed and how tall he was; he passed along Shirley's comment on his teeth, but said they were not all that good. He gave some figures that he guessed at on the taxicab business and asked George's opinion.

Then he wrote, "That must of been scary when the courthouse caught fire. And I am glad that that guy rescued you. You were lucky, because Dad sure can get hard about the least little thing. And burning the top out of the courthouse is kind of serious. Ha. Ha."

When he came to the end, Dave stalled. He stared out the window for a long time before he put down what he felt, hoping George would understand and forget about it before he came home; he wrote, "Love, David." Then he sealed and stamped the envelope and clothes-pinned it to the porch mailbox.

Dave worked out hard, slept an hour, and sat with the family until just before ten. He rode his bicycle down to the Eatwell and picked up Sue. As they were turning off Dyersburg, Ace Howard passed with the McLain House waitress everybody was getting into. Dave leaned forward so Ace could not see Sue.

When they got to Sue's house her parents were playing Monopoly on the living room rug. He and Sue got into the game long enough for Dave and Sergeant Wales to steal most of the bank's money. Sue's mother was banker. Whenever the oscillating fan swung, it agitated the money, and while she was distracted Dave and the sergeant took advantage of the bank.

The wind lifted the ten dollar bills, which were all that remained of the bank's assets. Mrs. Wales grabbed for them.

"Mother, Daddy took one of your houses off Atlantic Avenue and put it on his property," Sue charged.

"Cecil!" Mrs. Wales complained, as she tried to keep the ten dollar bills from blowing away.

"David, my only child accuses me of cheating."

"Don't talk to him. He is as crooked as you," Sue said.

"Now Cecil," Mrs. Wales warned, "I can't be banker if you're going to do that." She took one of the sergeant's houses and put it on Atlantic.

"I passed Go, Mrs. Wales, I get $200," Dave said as he took all the bank's tens.

"I did too." The sergeant recovered his house and seized $200 of Mrs. Wales' money.

"They did not," Sue shouted. "Neither one passed Go. Besides, David is in Jail and can't pass anything." Her face was that of a fourth-grade tattletale.

"If you tended to your business and stopped turning the players against one another you would have more than Baltic Avenue and the Reading Railroad," Dave said. He hooked an arm around her neck, but she struggled loose.

Mrs. Wales threw the dice. Her face fell as she landed on Ventnor Avenue, which the sergeant had improved with a hotel. She looked down and said, "Where is all my money?"

"Maybe you spent everything," Dave suggested.

"Cecil, you took it. That's not funny."

"Sell some houses," the sergeant advised.

"Cecil, I'll break your neck." She lunged at Sergeant Wales; he caught her and fell over laughing as she slapped at him. "I'll never play with you ever again." She struggled to free her arms to hit him and keep her skirt down.

174

Sue moved the fan out of the way. She leaned close to Dave, her face bright with excitement.

"You're just mean, Cecil. Now let me go. Cecil, let me go." She kicked, trying to get some leverage, and raked markers, houses, and hotels from the Monopoly board.

Finally, Sergeant Wales released her. She sat up, flushed, and tugging at her skirt. The sergeant winked at Dave. She ran her hand over her hair and looked at the board. "You made me do that." She slapped at him while keeping out of his reach. "You old mean thing."

"She sure is a hard loser, Sarge," Dave said.

"And you're mean too. You both cheat and do anything so nobody can tell who won." Mrs. Wales was on her feet straightening her dress.

Dave and Sue put the game away. Sergeant Wales sat on the couch grinning. His black hair was close-cropped, and he had deep laugh lines around his eyes. When Sue asked for the car he simply pitched the keys to her and kept watching Mrs. Wales, who was still denouncing him.

They drove by the square. Only a scattering of debris remained. The crane was gone. When Dave took Sue to see the truck, the two-by-twelves looked bigger than ever; Dave had thought maybe they would shrink, like the swelling going down after a broken arm was set. Sue did not laugh, which Dave appreciated. He held her close, wishing Cedric would see them, but the plant was deserted.

They did not go directly to Matson hill. Dave was not used to having cars entrusted to him out of hand; always there was time to plan what he would do with one. By the time they got to the hill, several cars were already parked, including Porky's. Dave ducked his head so he would not be recognized and drove to a stretch of abandoned pavement. He turned the radio to KRLD and helped Sue out of the car. "Here, wait a minute," he said. He knelt and took off her shoes, then balanced on one foot and with a hand on her shoulder, while he removed his own. He hung his socks on the vent glass. The pavement was still warm from the sun.

"Won't it run the battery down to leave the radio on?"

"Not for awhile."

Sue looked at their bare feet. "What is this for?"

"For dancing." He put his arm around her. They stood for a moment, then began moving with the music. "Sue, I want you for always."

"Yes," she said, and leaned her head against his chest.

The stretch of road was on the crest of a hill. On one side the lights of a distant farmhouse were visible. Dave wished there was a house like that where he and Sue lived. Later they had their first big fight. They were in the car, and she had moved his hand half a dozen times in just a few minutes. She stiffened and said they had better go home. He snatched his socks off the vent glass and threw them on the floor.

"What has got into you?" she demanded.

He fumbled with the ignition. The clutch pedal felt odd under his bare foot. "I don't know what you mean."

"You never acted like that before.

He had to step on the starter half a dozen times—scaring him that he had run the battery down — before the motor kicked over. "Is that right?"

"Yes, that's right."

"Well, you said you loved me, and I said I loved you."

"That doesn't mean you can do anything you have a mind to." She turned sideways in the seat and spread the skirt over her legs.

"You better lean off the goddam door if you don't want to end up in the road." He pushed the gas pedal down and turned off the radio.

"Don't you dare curse me." Her back was still against the door, but now she clutched the back of the seat for insurance.

"I'll say what I damn well please." They were getting louder and louder.

176

"Well, say it to Shirley."

He stared in disbelief; apparently everyone in the whole world knew about old Shirley. "Oh God. Who told you?"

"I know a lot more than I will ever tell."

He wished he had never seen Shirley or John Henry. She had brought him nothing but grief, and the slicker was the one who had gotten him mixed up with her.

"And you take the Lord's name in vain once more, I'll jump out."

He thought she was bluffing, but he was not sure.

"You have guilt written all over you," she stated.

"Not guilt with old Shirley, I'll guarantee."

"With somebody else?"

He fought the impulse to tell about Hazel. "I will only say that some women, one in particular that I can think of, chase after me."

The air in the car was thick with hostility all the way to town. As soon as they got to her house she flounced away, to stand under the porch light while he locked the car, as if she were afraid of him in the dark. He considered pitching the keys to her, but did not for the same reason she did not flounce all the way into the house. He gave her the keys and a sterile kiss. "Tell Sarge thanks."

He waited for her to say or do something. "Well, I'll see you around." He sat on the sidewalk and put on his shoes.

Her lips were pursed and her eyes cold.

"I guess I'll never drive it again." Dave gazed at the car as if it were an old friend about to move to Denver.

"Is that what you want?"

"No, but it's the way you want it to be."

They stared at each other. Dave kicked up the stand on the bicycle and she said with fresh fury, "You aren't going to tell me?"

"About what?"

"About Shirley what's-her-name, that's what."

He would not have believed her capable of such anger.

"I haven't seen her since the first time I walked you home."

"That is not what I heard."

"You heard wrong then." He tried to sound so indignant that she would be afraid to give him any more trouble.

They spent fifteen minutes saying, "I got to go" and "I got to go in" until there was nothing to do but go and go in. Dave made a peace overture. "We going to the show Saturday?"

"We will see," she said icily.

His temper flared. He should have known better than to act the Christian. "Awrighty, righty, we will just see. Call and let me know." He swung aboard the bicycle and pumped hard. As he reached the corner he turned his head to hear what she was shouting.

"You are vile," she yelled. "VILE, VILE, VILE."

He rode furiously up the hill, wondering if there was a single person he had not gotten crossways with that day.

11

All the way to the plant Dave hoped Mr. Blackstone had already seen the bumpers. Maybe he would be resigned to the two-by-twelves before Dave finished his route. He had delivered two loads before the old man got to work; the first came out the front door, but he took the other over the back dock. He did not want to be present when Daddy Warbucks saw the bumpers for the first time. He could visualize those old hands dragging him out of the truck by his T-shirt.

Elmo was still giving him the cold treatment; Dave had planned to pretend he did not notice Elmo's juvenile behavior, but that was too much of a burden when he had to worry about being manhandled by his employer. He put his boot on the running board and said, "What are you all puffed up about?"

The hick seemed bewildered. "Son, you change directions like a weather rooster."

"Good Lord, Elmo, I forgave you for the rotten things you said about old Shirley's picture. And I haven't said a word about that trashy pillow and your crap in the glove compartment. Not to mention that Folger's coffee can that you don't empty out near often enough. And I have not brought up that you took the door off and probably warped the frame."

Elmo saw Dave looking at the open glove compartment

179

and slammed the door. After they got the third load on the truck Dave went in to use the telephone. He was gone only a few minutes, but when he came back he found a wide strip of fresh white paint down the back cushion and across the seat, separating the helper's side from the iceman's. Elmo was perched on his pillow as if nothing had happened.

Dave exploded. "That is the most childish thing I have ever seen, besides which it is more damage to Friendly property."

Elmo was disdainful. The pillow raised him so high his hat almost touched the ceiling.

"Daddy Warbucks has got his eye on this truck because you took the door off. And don't think I will stick up for you when he asks about the seat painting."

From then on Elmo refused to speak to Dave; all communication was by hand signal. "I don't believe nobody could act this way," Dave would say, "and especially not a forty-two year old man with a boy overseas."

Elmo would spit in the coffee can.

About eleven o'clock Dave took a hundred pounds into the little gin. He was coming down the outside stairs when Elmo yelled; Dave took the steps three at a time and found Elmo standing in the truck bed holding his wrist with an ice pick stuck clear through his hand. There was no blood on the back of the hand and only a drop or two in his palm. "Hold still," Dave ordered as he grabbed Elmo's wrist, took a deep breath, and pulled. The point grated on bone as it came out, raising chill bumps on Dave's arms.

Elmo slung his hand and grimmaced.

"Get in the cab and mash till it bleeds. We're going to the doctor."

Elmo gestured wildly as Dave made a U-turn and sped away.

"For Pete's sake, stop being stupid and talk."

Elmo made some more signs.

Dave said, "No, he won't give you a tetanus shot unless you need it."

There were more signals and some noises that sounded as if Elmo were swallowing his chew.

"No, you won't get swole up neither. Mrs. O'Konski was just allergic."

The noises became guttural and fire burned in Elmo's eyes.

"I don't care what you say," Dave answered, "getting swole up is better than lockjaw."

Elmo growled and indicated that he would jump.

Dave sighed. Not only did everyone get angry with him, but eventually they all threatened to jump out of a car. "Well, die with your jaw froze then. You don't talk anyhow."

When they stopped at the Sinclair station, Dave warned, "You better mash some blood out." He bought a Dr. Pepper for the hick, who set it on the open glove compartment door and nodded in thanks. He unsnapped a narrow coin purse and offered a nickle to Dave.

"You know what you can do with that nickle," Dave said, promising not to do any more nice things for ingrates. He noticed white paint smeared on his levis, and added, "You simple hillbilly."

When they returned to the plant Daddy Warbucks' car was parked in front of the machinery room; Dave dared him to say something about the bumpers. Everyone would be well advised not to mess with him. The helper had his legs crossed and was cradling his wounded hand while he chewed tobacco and drank Dr. Pepper. "Forty-two year old idiot," Dave grumbled, wheeling into the dock so anyone in the office would have to notice, bumpers, seat, and all.

When Daddy Warbucks did not appear Dave went to the machinery room so he could look into the office. Mr. Blackstone, in a rope-bottomed chair, was talking to two strangers in business suits and one in boots and a ten-gallon hat. The cowboy was at the old man's desk. Dave could not figure it out.

John Henry came in from his next-to-last trip and was

sitting on the dock watching Elmo knead the hand. Elmo still had not drawn a whole drop of blood. Dave made the Indian sign for "go home," and Elmo left.

"What's with him?" John Henry said.

Dave leaned against the wall with his arms crossed. "He ain't speaking. He's mad at me. Everybody but you is."

Just then O. P. drove up, and the office emptied. One stranger was in front of the truck and one on the passenger's side. When the cowboy hauled out the struggling O. P., Dave and John Henry came off the dock running. Daddy Warbucks stepped in front of them. "Get your routes finished up," he ordered.

"Hi, Mr. Blackstone," John Henry said.

The old man hurried away.

Dave said, "I'm already through. Let's load you and see what's happening."

They took their time, easing about the dock and watching O. P. and the strangers. O. P.'s hands were over his head and one of the men was turning his pockets wrong-side out.

"I seen this picture show oncet where . . . ."

"Shut up," Dave said.

The old man came toward them again. They pretended to straighten the tarp.

"Hi, Mr. Blackstone," John Henry said.

"Totten."

"Yes sir."

"Where's Elmo?"

"Gone home. He stuck an ice pick through his hand."

"Well, you two will have to finish O. P.'s route." The strangers were struggling to put O. P. into a black Ford.

"I just wonder what he did," John Henry said into the old man's ear.

Mr. Blackstone, seeming not to have heard, went slowly back to the office.

"What did O. P. do?" John Henry demanded of Dave.

"How should I know?"

182

"Why didn't you ask?"

"Why didn't you?"

"I did."

"You did not. You just mooned around wondering out loud."

"That was asking."

"It was not. Asking is saying, 'Mr. Blackstone, you old bastard, what did they pick O. P. up for?' "

Dave helped John Henry finish his route, then they spent two hours following the rough list in O. P.'s faded Five Year Diary. The deliveries did not take that long; most of the time was taken up talking about O. P. Elmer Lipscomb thought O. P. was a Jap spy. Mrs. Norbert Paley figured Franklin Roosevelt had heard some of the nasty things O. P. said about the WPA. Mrs. Eula Suggs stated that O. P. had an extra wife and kids off somewhere and he was not supporting them since he could not look a woman in the eye without smiling.

They were using Dave's truck because it was easier to get in and out. John Henry was so preoccupied with O. P.'s problem that he had not asked about the paint on the seat.

"O. P. has a miserable route," Dave remarked. "I haven't seen anything but hillbillies and beer drinkers and wrestling fans and holy rollers."

"Mrs. Hoskins is on your route and her and her husband are hillbillies."

Dave was irritated. Mrs. Hoskins always asked about George, and she never left her butter and stuff so Dave had to move it. "They are different."

"Just because they're your customers don't make them different."

"I'm tired of you contradicting me all the time," Dave said, knowing he should pitch out both John Henry and Elmo's pillow.

"You know when O. P. ran off from that extra wife and kids . . . ."

"Just shut up." Dave was ashamed of all the talking they had done about O. P. At the blacksmith shop John Henry announced that O. P. had four kids in Grayson County — one with the rickets — and was not sending them any money. As they left Dave said, "O. P. is going to be back tomorrow, and he is going to punch hell out of you. And I will hold his coat and lead the cheers."

They finished the route and hurried back to the plant to learn the latest development. Levi Hackley was out front talking to Cedric and Daddy Warbucks. A few feet away stood Red Fick with a satchel hanging from his shoulder and the big camera he used to cover football games for the *Caller-Times*.

John Henry's eyes got big. "O. P. must have held up a bank. *Fortune* magazine says there's lots of that going on."

Mr. Blackstone motioned for Dave to stop and came toward the truck at a fast clip, his faded blue trousers hanging from a slack belt.

"Hi, Mr. Blackstone," John Henry said.

"David, stop in front of the office and head the truck toward the street."

Levi Hackley crouched and signalled as if Dave were landing on an aircraft carrier. Dave ignored Levi; he switched off the ignition and yelled at Cedric, "What's up?"

"Just taking some pictures."

As Dave got out of the truck — and for the first and only time in his life — Daddy Warbucks shook his hand. "David," he said, "this is Levi Hackley."

"Totten." Hackley touched the brim of his pork-pie hat and acted as if he did not know Dave.

"This is John Henry Panky," Dave said, not sure why he did that; they had known each other all their lives.

Levi flipped the hat brim again. "Fine young lad. Member of our church, where I organized the youth choir." He turned away and began giving instructions to Fick.

"That son-of-a-bitch," John Henry said with enough volume to cause Mr. Blackstone's usual expression to become even more dour, "he is only two years older than me."

Fick, sucking on a wet-ended cigarette, ignored Levi. His shirt tail was coming out of his trousers and both shoestrings were untied.

Levi said, "Totten, you up here. Mr. Blackstone, your arm around his shoulders. You, Panky, on the other side, and I'll put my arm around you." John Henry was surly as he took his place. Hackley stopped to admire the arrangement. "Just fine. Great morale thing for the homefront as well as our boys across the water. He draped his arm over John Henry. "Does the bumper show all right, Red?"

Fick's only response was to click the shutter and wind the film.

Levi said, "I wish we had our banner here. Slap-a-Jap with a bumper, huh, Mr. Blackstone?"

John Henry made a face as if he would throw up.

"Now, let's get Mr. Blackstone in front of the truck with me, as chairman of the scrap drive, shaking his hand. Totten can be by the fender. You get away, Panky."

As Dave moved to the fender his pencil fell from behind his ear and he bent to pick it up. When he turned back around, Fick was putting a lid over the lens of the camera.

"That's it," Hackley announced.

"Did he take a picture?" Dave asked, but no one seemed to hear.

Levi shook hands all around, then buzzed off, with Fick loitering behind.

"Good work, Totten," Daddy Warbucks said. He drove away in the Oldsmobile.

Dave walked into the office, dazed.

"Red Fick got a great shot of your butt, Hotshot," Cedric said.

"What were those pictures for?"

Before Cedric could answer, John Henry interrupted to ask about O. P.

"They're going to put the bumper thing in the paper, Hotshot. And O. P. has been playing hide-and-seek with the draft board."

"Well damn, Ced, they took everybody else's picture, too. It was me that made the donation."

Cedric smirked and took out his Bull Durham sack and cigarette papers. "You was the only one showing their butt though."

"I'm going to bust Levi Hackley in the mouth. Red Fick, too." Dave looked up the *Caller-Times'* phone number. "I got to call and give my side or the paper's gonna say Levi Hackley give them bumpers and Levi accepted them."

While Cedric and John Henry speculated on O. P.'s future Dave talked to old man Peery at the newspaper. He was relieved when he hung up. Then it occurred to him that the bad photograph might appear with the story. "Aw, they wouldn't do that," he said.

"Do what, Hotshot?" Cedric talked around the cigarette, which looked like something Ellis might make from leaves and toilet paper and flour paste.

"Nothin." All the riff-raff Dave knew smoked cigarettes.

Later Dave used the newspaper story as an excuse to call Sue. She was cool at first, but everything came out right. He could take her home from work, and they would go to the show Saturday if the Lyric's air conditioning were fixed.

He went with John Henry to get the hamburgers even though he won the toss. He did not trust the slicker's big mouth, which was probably how Sue learned about old Shirley. Dave leaned on the cigar counter and talked to Sue while Theo and John Henry argued about O. P. being hauled off. "They could of wrote him a letter," John Henry said.

Theo pointed to the soldiers in the back booth. "All other men go. You be gone. I go but that I am sixty." Theo bent and groped beneath the counter for a set of smudged and grease-stained citizenship papers that he showed customers several times a day.

"I seen them papers three hundred times, Theo," John Henry complained. "And what you say ain't democratic."

Theo's booming voice filled the whole cafe. "Democratic. Americans invent democratic?" He held up the documents.

"I say I seen them damn papers, Theo."

"Greeks invent democratic."

"All you wops believe that old country stuff."

In the hostile silence that followed Dave hustled John Henry and the hamburgers to the truck. He stopped at the hardware store for paint and later used a catsup bottle top to draw circles on the bumpers, which he painted white with red polka dots. He found Elmo's door hidden in the machinery room and washed off the tobacco juice with a garden hose.

"He won't like that," John Henry warned as Dave put the helper's door on the truck.

"I am the captain of this truck. Besides which he has O. P.'s route now."

The clean door made the rest of the truck look bad, so John Henry helped him wash the whole thing. Then Dave drove it downtown for Dad to see, although some of the red paint had run onto the white and John Henry had gotten the back bumper wet.

"I see you got paint on your pants leg," Dad said.

"Yes sir." Dave was wearing yesterday's levis; he was grateful that Dad had not seen the seat stripe.

Dave shot two games of snooker with John Henry, who barely won but was terribly overbearing.

"One day somebody's going to mash you like a bug, Slicker. Somebody like Theo."

"Huh. I'd like to see that."

"You better watch what you call people. Greeks aren't wops."

"Greasers, then. Me and Patsy are getting married Tuesday right after work, so the license office won't be closed. And we're counting on you."

187

"You can't take Patsy with you when you go into the army."

"I got to, Dave. Nobody ever loved anybody like me and Patsy do one another."

Dave got distracted by the simple look on John Henry's face and missed the wild ball, costing him six points and the game.

That afternoon Dinty died. Dave and Ellis buried him back of the tree house, then Dave went to George's room, scotched the door knob with a chair, and cried. He tried to write George about the old bulldog, but he could not.

The rest of the week was peaceful enough. It was hard getting used to being without Dinty. George was on Dave's mind more and more. Dave's bumpers still got a lot of attention. He had traded Pendleton Street to John Henry for Railroad Avenue. On the second day the slicker said, "That black-headed woman on Pendleton wanted me to dance with her," which made Dave angry and then sad.

Elmo did fine with O. P.'s route, although Dave figured he probably had to drag anything over fifty pounds. His customers called him T-Bone, and he still hung his hooks from his hip pocket. His new lunch bucket had been varnished to preserve the picture of Br'er Rabbit carrying the pancakes. He and Dave got along as splendidly as if they had never been closely associated. Elmo switched from Brown's Mule to Days Work on Dave's recommendation.

On Thursday Mary went to a dance at the VFW with Dave and Sue, and he felt easier about George. There was a blanket party on Friday night; he got Sue's clothes off and they talked about getting married. She cried, and he got upset about her and Dinty and George and wept, too.

The *Caller-Times* ran the bumper picture — not the one with Dave picking up the pencil — and a story about the donation. Mr. Blackstone looked terribly old in the photograph. Mother sent a copy of the paper to George.

O. P. had been assigned to a special camp for riff-raff. The army would send him overseas as soon as he could handle a rifle. Everyone said O. P. was lucky he had no federal penitentiary time to do.

More and more Dave considered joining the army. He would be seventeen soon and most of his friends were gone. John Henry would go soon. Dave did not mention the army to Sue anymore. She always accused him of wanting to get away from her and said it was enough that her father was in the army.

On Saturday afternoon Dave drove the sergeant's car down to the stadium and ran laps while Sue lay in the shade of the bleachers poring over a *Reader's Digest*. He jogged over to her and flopped on the beach towel she had spread in the tall grass.

She put the magazine down. "How far was that?"

"About four miles," he said, exaggerating. Still breathing hard, he rolled over on his back and put his arms behind his head.

She took up the magazine again and began to read out loud an Ernie Pyle story about a Captain Waskow, from Texas. The sky was light blue and the clouds were soft and loose. In the east Dave thought he saw the glint of a star. Sue read of the good captain and the way his men brought him back dead and how they felt. Ever since Dave was thinking about throwing the *Fort Worth Press* he had read Ernie Pyle's stuff.

Dave's breathing was normal again. The good tiredness spread along his thighs and calves and the bottoms of his feet burned everywhere there was a cleat; he needed new innersoles. When she finished he said, "Waskow don't sound very Texas, but Ernie Pyle wouldn't write it if it wasn't true."

Sue's eyes were misty; she got sad easy. He took her small hand and said, "Is that a star over there?"

Although they were in the shade, she put her free hand above her eyes. "I don't know."

"Your mother and Sarge, they get along good."

She did not answer.

"My folks do, too, but they don't live as easy as yours."
He was quiet for a long while. "Sue, we would always live
in Texas."

"All right."

"No beaches, no mountains, just plain country."

"Okay."

"Because I couldn't live anywhere else. We been here
a hundred years. Grandpa's grandpa got himself hung
down in the county during the Civil War." He got up,
measuring his energy. "Let me do one more and we'll go."
He forced his tired muscles into a slow jog. Sue drove him
home so he did not have to take off the football shoes. He
and Porky would call for her at seven.

Dave and the family were listening to the Hit Parade
when Porky came for him. Dad groused about the music,
claiming Gene Austin's "Blue Heaven" was the last decent
song ever written. Dave was chewing Ten Crown Activated
Charcoal Gum to take off some of the tobacco stain; Dad
gave him a hard look as a reminder that he did not approve
of gum chewing.

They had to leave early, so if the Lyric were still closed
they could go to a movie in Denton and still get in some
heavy courting. The Lyric was Lawton's only decent
theater; the others were foot-and-onion places that showed
only westerns on Saturday.

Sarge was in the living room when they got to Sue's
house. Porky was about half scared of him. Sarge said,
"Sue was all ready until she saw you come up."

"Cecil!" Mrs. Wales said. "Talk about something else."
Betty and Mrs. Wales went back to Sue's room. After
awhile Sue came in looking awfully nice. They went straight
to the Lyric. Porky double-parked while Dave checked
with the cashier. Dave trotted back and opened the rear
door, saying, "Take off, Porky, Speedy Thomas is around
the corner."

190

Porky pulled away from the curb while Dave fell into the back seat. "The air conditioner is on, and they start selling tickets in a half hour. There's a trailer about a bomber squadron."

They bought cherry cokes at the drugstore and got in the line that had formed outside the Lyric; it extended the length of the block. Sue was wearing a white dress with a pleated skirt; Dave kept his arm around her and introduced her to half the town. When Porky started tickling Betty, Dave tried to act as if he did not know them.

Inside, Dave took an aisle seat so he could stretch his legs. Sue and Betty sat between him and Porky. The theater filled as the previews ran and was packed by the time the feature came on. It was a pirate movie. The audience, half of which was soldiers, cheered throughout, especially during the sword fights.

Dave got the candy and popcorn so Porky would not step on their feet. Porky kept leaning past Betty to make remarks he thought were funny; Dave wished he would quit. In the last scene the pirate hero returned and asked the girl to marry him. Sue got a little weepy and squeezed Dave's hand.

When the newsreel showed former Vice President Garner at his Uvalde home, the soldiers booed and stamped their feet at the mention of Texas.

Porky was enraged. "Why don't they go back where they come from?" he complained.

"The army won't let them," Sue answered, and Dave was proud of her.

The short subject came on and the narrator began describing a day he spent with a bomber squadron in England. He followed the activities of the group, showing them at meals, playing volleyball, going to classes, and preparing for a mission.

"That's what George does," Dave whispered. Sue leaned her head against his shoulder.

The camera showed a long line of bombers being warmed

up in a misting rain. Then the narrator talked to the crews, having each man state his name and hometown. Some of the soldiers in the audience cheered each time a place was mentioned, unless it was in Texas; then they all booed. Porky could not stand it; he got into an argument with two soldiers sitting next to him and it looked as if one would clean Porky's plow. Dave wished they would postpone their disagreement.

Then there appeared on the screen a tall youngish, oldish man wearing a flight jacket and a cap with no grommet and many missions in the crown. The camera moved on to his crew.

Dave gasped. "That was George," he said. "Sue, that's George at the end there." He leaned forward and strained to hear as the crew members introduced themselves. Dave knew some of them from George's letters. Then the camera came in close on George. He was very thin, and there was a tired sadness in his eyes, but he smiled when he said, "First Lieutenant George F. Totten, Lawton, Texas."

The response of the soldiers was deafening, which irritated Dave. It was one thing to boo strangers, but disrespect toward George was just not right even though George would get a kick out of it when Dave wrote him.

Porky was trying to get his attention, but Dave ignored him as the crew members picked up their parachutes and clambered into the plane. George was the last to enter. He glanced to his right, as if someone were telling him to do something, then he turned, smiled sadly, waved, and was gone.

Dave swallowed hard. "God, I'll be glad when he's home." He buried his face in Sue's hair.

There was no sense staying any longer. Porky kept after Dave, and friends were coming from all over the theater to talk to him. People sitting nearby were getting peeved, and Dave did not blame them. He and Sue went out into the lobby until Porky finished seeing Woody Woodpecker. As they went to the car Dave felt better than he had in months. George was well and would be home before long. It was good to be alive in George's town; with his arm around Sue he walked down the middle of Ash Street sing-ing — yelling, really — the "Wabash Cannonball." Near the end he did a little buck and wing he had learned for a minstrel show when he was in the third grade. They piled into Porky's car laughing and shouting at each other.

Porky said, "Where to?"

"Anywhere," Dave said, then thought better of it. "No, I got to tell the folks. Stop at the ice house and I'll call home."

Just before they got to the plant Dave said, "My trouble was that I forgot that the war would be over one day." He took Sue into the empty office and kissed her before and after Central took the number.

Ellis answered.

"Buddy Boy, let me talk to Mother."

"David, you come on home."

The line went dead, and Dave laughed. "It was Ellis. He hung up on me."

"What did they say?" Porky yelled from the car. For some reason he still had the motor running.

"Ellis hung up on him," Sue said.

They all laughed; Dave thought it was the funniest thing that ever happened. He would write George about that, too. They went through the kissing routine again while Central rang.

"Ellis," Dave said to the little brother, "I told you I wanted to talk to Mother."

"You are supposed to come on home."

"Don't hang up on me," Dave shouted as the receiver went down.

Everyone laughed again, more than before. Ellis really needed his tail kicked, but Dave just could not be angry now. Dave apologized to the operator, had her ring again, said said, "Sue, I'm going to work him over like George used to threaten to do me."

The receiver was raised, but Dave did not recognize the voice. He put his hand over the mouthpiece and told the others, "I got a wrong number now."

Porky honked the horn and gunned the engine. Betty was hysterical. Sue held her hand over her mouth as she always did when something was funny. Whoever answered kept trying to get Dave to talk, which made it more hilarious to Dave. When he could stop laughing long enough, he said, "I'm sorry, I was calling the Totten residence, ma'am." He made faces at the others.

Then the voice said, "This is the Totten residence."

"Well, this is David Totten. Who are you?" Dave was dizzy and scared.

The voice hesitated. "This is Mrs. Barkley."

"Dr. Barkley's wife?"

"David, I think you ought to come on home."

He fell back against the wall, pulling Sue with him. "Don't hang up on me, Mrs. Barkley," he pleaded. "Is anything wrong?"

"Yes, David."

He could not bear whatever it was. "It's Mother, isn't it?"

"No, it's George."

He collapsed into Mr. Blackstone's swivel chair. Sue was kneeling beside him and Porky, looking stunned, hung out of the car window with the motor still going. Nothing moved anywhere in the world. "Is he missing in action, Mrs. Barkley?"

"No, David. George is dead."

Sue took the receiver and put it in the cradle; she was weeping. Porky and Betty and the car seemed frozen. Sue's white skirt was touching the dirty concrete floor. Dave ran his fingers through her black hair. She was very fragile; she would not outweigh Mary by five pounds. Dave heard Porky's motor and Sue's crying. He felt her head against his thigh and her hair in his hand. The walls and ceiling were varnished yellow pine with knots which were reddish

194

on the edges and dark brown — as if they were decayed — in the center. A bare light bulb dangled from a kinked wire.

Then Dave was whimpering and praying and cursing. Sue was begging him not to swear, and he was trying to tell her he knew it was wrong and did not mean it but was swearing anyway. Because George was dead, and there was nothing to be done about it. And there was left in the whole brown world only Mary and Ellis and Mother and Dad and Sue and him.

Sunday morning Ellis came into George's room and crawled into bed with Dave. "I got the paper, David. George is in it."

Dave rolled over on his back. The sun was out warm and new; it was not too hot yet. "Hi, Buddy Boy." Dave spread his arm, and Ellis used it for a pillow.

"See." The little brother shoved the paper in Dave's face.

The picture had been made when George was in flight training, when he was smooth-faced and there was nothing sad or tired about him.

"How come you stayed in George's room?"

"President Roosevelt told me to."

Ellis got up on his knees and started to pounce. "He did not."

Dave held up an arm to fend Ellis off. "No, he didn't. No rasslin, now. You just lay here. Maybe you can sleep some more."

Dave read a little of the newspaper story and stared at the photograph. He let the paper fall to the floor.

"I'm not going to Sunday School."

"No." Dave's head ached and his eyes burned. Last night at the ice plant seemed years ago. He was over it all, except for not seeing how anything could ever be worthwhile again.

"You're not going either?"

"None of us are."

"I cried because George is dead."

"Me, too." Dave was glad the day had come. All night long, whenever he slept, he had watched George, tired and sad, wave and climb into an airplane.

"George is going to heaven."

"Uh huh." Dave fought the tears again. Someone was moving about downstairs.

Ellis lay with his head on Dave's shoulder, his legs crossed and the pajamas reaching just below his knee; he had grown some while no one noticed. "Will George come here first?"

"What do you mean?"

"On the way to heaven."

"He's already gone." Dave looked at his brother. "You understand?"

Ellis nodded quickly and bounced his leg.

"We won't see him again, Buddy Boy, until we go to heaven, too." Dave jumped up and ran to his own room. After awhile he dried his eyes and came back. "Let's make up George's bed. Then we'll do yours. We got to be real nice to Mother today."

"I know."

After Dave was ready he got Ellis into his good suit and took him down to the bathroom.

"How come I'm dressed up if I'm not going to Sunday School?"

"We're going to the picture show that George is in." He combed Ellis' hair using some of George's good stuff.

Ellis' chin began to quiver. "I part it on the other side."

"Can you get along with it this way just this once?"

"Uh huh," the little boy said, and began sobbing.

Dave sat on the side of the tub and comforted Ellis; he put the part where it was supposed to be and washed Ellis' face. Then they went into the kitchen.

"I'm hungry," Ellis said. He took his place across from

196

Dad, who sat at the table as if he had always been there.

Dave spoke to Mrs. Barkley and the other neighbor. He held Mother for a minute and touched Dad's shoulder. His father seemed so old and helpless; Dave did not think he could stand it. "I'll go get Mary and Grandpa and Grandma."

"Won't you have some breakfast?" one of the neighbors said, and Dave knew it would be cowardly to leave those two old people and those strangers and that shined-up little boy. He sat down and ate as little as he could without worrying Mother, but he stayed until only he and Ellis remained at the table. Then he went out to the garage, ran a rag over the car, and wept at the mound of new dirt back of the tree house.

He backed out of the gravel driveway. Sue would meet him at the theater; except for her, only the family would be present. Dave looked at himself in the rearview mirror and wondered if he would become more like George as he got older. He was already sweating the white shirt; it was going to be a long day.

Dave made his route on Monday and Tuesday and finished early on Wednesday; the memorial services were at two. Instead of being almost gone, as he had thought, Dave's grief and that he could see in his parents built day by day. Mrs. Wales said it worked that way, but after the services the pain would start to go away.

Sue sat with him at the church. Afterward Grandma broke down and they almost had to carry her to the car. Dave went back to thank the preacher, and Levi Hackley and the American Legion commander met him midway up the church steps. The legionnaire was a short, earnest veteran of World War I. He was holding a gold star window flag that he had brought for the Tottens. He started to present it to Dave and stumbled over his memorized speech.

Levi took the flag from him, said some unctuous things and handed it to Dave. As Levi continued talking about "our gold star mothers" and "our fallen heroes" Dave suddenly lost control. He half hit, half pushed, Levi, who fell two steps before he caught himself. "You don't own this war, Levi," Dave shouted and ran into the church.

Dave and Ellis left with Sue's parents. Mrs. Wales, with pencil and paper, tried to entertain Ellis in the back seat. Sue sat between Dave and Sarge, who was driving. Dave kissed Sue on the forehead, then slammed his fist down on the dash, crying, "Oh, God damn."

Mrs. Wales squeezed his arm and said, "It will pass, David."

He pulled Sue to him.

"Mrs. Wales, David cussed," Ellis said in a loud whisper, "and he hit a man."

12

The family drifted through the days following the service. Ellis changed the least of any of them. Mother kept her thoughts to herself; although it was July she wore a sweater over her shoulders as she sat in the living room of an evening. Dad seemed too tired to be irritable anymore.

Dave kept thinking he would come home from work one day and find George in his room with his leg draped over the chair arm. Dave was having to give up his plans. All of the stories he was saving, all the ideas he wanted to share, he was letting slip from his memory. Now George would remember him as a little kid, and Dave regretted that terribly. The main chore for all of them was realizing that there was no one else; they were four now.

The telegram was still on the mantel where it had been laid that Saturday evening. One day when he was alone Dad put the gold flag in the front window; everyone pretended not to notice.

Nothing in Lawton had changed much. The grass had lost most of its green to the middle summer heat. Seventeen German prisoners escaped and were found camped in an abandoned saddle shop at Dyersburg. Levi Hackley was running for mayor on the strength of the successful scrap drive. John Henry spent a month's pay on a bracelet for Patsy. "Elmer's Tune" had been put on the nickelodeon at Jiggs West's Cafe and the hillbillies thought it was brand new and played it all the time. And Cedric told Dave about Warren's having had a picture of George on his wall ever since George made All State. Dave decided Warren was among the outstanding boys in Lawton High School.

One day as John Henry was loading out, he said, "Hey, guess what happened, Dave?"

"Daddy Warbucks' pants got stole and a burglar is holding them for $8,000 ransom."

"I mean really."

"What?"

"O. P. deserted from the army."

"He hasn't been in long enough to desert."

"I think they ought to catch all the people they already have before they draft any new ones," John Henry said.

Cedric, chewing a match and fiddling with his clipboard, came in. "Hotshot, you and your brother-in-law there must of give up watermelon? We ain't had a theft in two weeks."

"You got some bad manners is all I can say," John Henry told him in a reasonable tone.

Cedric smirked. He started out, then said, "Oh yeah, you got a letter, Hotshot." He slipped an envelope out from beneath the papers on the clipboard. Dave thanked him and stuffed it into his hip pocket. When he got to the truck he studied the handwriting; there was no return address, but he knew it was from Hazel. He drove to the far corner of the park and opened the blue envelope, addressed to him at "The Ice Plant on Kentuckytown Avenue."

The letter was written in pencil on stationery with flowers and birds across the top; Dave had bought Mother a box of that at the five and dime one Christmas.

"Dear David," it said in a ninth grade scrawl, "Ted is shipped out and I am now back at home. But I saw the photo of your brother in the Lawton paper before I left. I never knew your last name until I saw how much you favored him and that he had a brother named David. I didn't know what to write you about it, but I wanted you to know how bad I felt. He reminded me of somebody I

200

knew once. I wish things had been different, for I know we will not see one another again in this life. But I will always be, Your — Hazel."

Dave read it several times and his eyes got full of tears, which happened quite often now. Then he tore the letter and envelope into tiny pieces and scattered them on the ground. He opened the glove compartment with the key Elmo had left in the lock and examined the contents. He shredded Shirley's picture and threw away her earrings and the other stuff that had accumulated, including Elmo's coffee can.

Dave leaned against the sideboards of the truck, listening to the wind in the trees, and watching two kids with fishing poles wade the waist-high grass across the creek. It was hot and bright, like any other summer Texas day. The sun came down hard on the fishermen and their cane poles, but everything seemed slower and darker than before. The wind caught pieces of Hazel's letter, took them a short way, dropped them, then came again, carrying them always away from him. Dave took a chew of Days Work, then spat it out and pitched the plug into the grass. Speedy Thomas drove by, and Dave acted as if he were working on the truck.

He visited Grandpa and Grandma that afternoon. Dave heard again, and tried to commit to memory, the story of how his great-great grandfather, Simeon Totten, was hanged in the second year of the Civil War. Dave told about George being in the courthouse fire and Archer pulling him out. The only Archer either remembered was an ancient black man who sold vegetables door to door when Grandpa was a boy.

Grandma warned Dave that chile and milk curdled in the stomach and caused a sure and painful death. She was embroidering dish towels and pondering other hazards, when John Henry blew in, needing to talk.

Dave and John Henry went over to the Dutch Inn and sat in the back booth while Darla, recently returned from

Tulsa, took their order. It turned out that John Henry was heartbroken; he unburdened himself about Patsy at great length and with much repetition. Darla, seeming older, brought their hamburgers and John Henry asked for catsup, which Dave considered a good sign of his ability to handle problems. Finally Dave said, "Well Slicker, there's nothing to do but forget her."

"But everything was going so good. I had the rings and bracelet, and you were going to sign." John Henry doused the hamburger with catsup.

"Maybe she couldn't help it. I saw that old mother of hers, and I sure wouldn't want to go up against her."

John Henry wagged his head sadly. "No. It wasn't nothin like that. Her folks just said if she wouldn't marry me she could have an all expense paid vacation to Missouri by bus. I really got mad. I said, 'Patsy, if you don't care no more about me than that I'd be well shut of you'."

"Well, she promised that she wouldn't go. But I come by this afternoon and she's took a bus for Missouri. So I went over and saw Shirley and found out that Patsy had been plotting for four or five days to go. Furthermore, Patsy said some damnable things about me, which I had to pull out of Shirley." John Henry gazed into space and sighed. "Shirley sure has been good to me in all this."

"What's in Missouri?"

"Some damn bat caves, or a place where Jesse James hid out, or something."

Dave studied the design on the new menu and decided somebody had traced the woman off a can of Old Dutch Cleanser. "That's it then, Slicker. You couldn't take her back after she has gone to Missouri on you."

John Henry was lost in thought. He folded one of the new menus into an airplane. "Shirley says I got to pick up the pieces and start a whole new life. Her and me are going out dancing tonight and talk about it some more. You don't care, do you?"

202

"No, No," Dave said. "It's good that Shirley's helpin you out."

John Henry held the airplane at arm's length, admired it, and checked its balance. "You didn't tell Shirley about Patsy's skivvies somehow happening to be in my car?"

"Lord no."

"Well that's good. I didn't think you did, but I wouldn't want her having any wrong ideas."

"Shirley's a great girl," Dave said.

"Yeah, she really is. It's funny that I never noticed until now. Patsy was so beautiful she had me kind of blinded."

"Probably."

"But Shirley is a whole lot more beautiful than Patsy in lots of ways," John Henry said.

When they got outside, John Henry launched the airplane. It traveled forward only a couple of feet then went straight down and crumpled its nose on the asphalt.

Almost a week later Dave went by the Eatwell on one of Sue's nights off. Theo was mopping the floor, since the swamper quit to go to the bomber plant in Fort Worth. He sat down with Dave long enough to give his latest opinion of John Henry. Ace Howard was sitting at the counter drinking coffee. The white shirt set off his tan and gunfighter moustache. Dave was glad Sue was not there. When Theo began mopping in front of the counter, Ace got up and came toward Dave carrying his cup.

"Are you David Totten?"

Dave shook his hand and offered him a chair.

Ace sat at an angle to the table with his legs crossed. "It's funny how you know who people are in a small town but you don't know them." He did not look as evil up close as from a distance. His teeth were white and even. "I was sorry about George. We graduated together."

"I didn't know that."

"You remember those coveralls with Lawton High School and a lion on the back. We had some made at the same time. He got mine by mistake, and they almost cut him in two. And I got his and they were like a sack."

Dave laughed and felt better than he had in several days. He decided to wear those coveralls when the weather got cooler.

"And George and I ran Coach Gallagher's shorts up the flagpole one day when we came in early from workout and he was still on the field. I still have not seen anything so ugly; they were yellow and green and you know Coach must of been sixty inches around the waist. And we got in a hell of a mess at the courthouse that I'll tell you about." He gulped the coffee, shook Dave's hand, and winked. "But I got to meet someone now."

Dave stared at the empty coffee cup for a long time, thinking Ace might be a better guy if he shaved off that moustache. He went up to the cigar counter and called home.

"Mother, is George's high school annual handy?"

"Which year?"

"Any of them. His senior annual."

She was gone for a minute. "I have it."

"Turn to George's class and see if there is a picture of an Ace Howard."

He heard her explaining to Ellis what she was doing. After awhile she said, "No."

"Are there any Howards at all? Read me whatever there are."

"There's Anne Howard. I went to school with her mother. Her grandfather was the first person I ever knew who had a car."

"Is that all?"

"Except for Archer."

"Archer? What does Archer look like?"

"He is very dark and has black hair and lovely teeth."

Although it was after eight when he got to Sue's house, she was still getting dressed. He followed Mrs. Wales back to the kitchen. "Where's Sarge?"

"He has charge of quarters tonight."

Dave pushed aside a picnic basket and sat down at the dinette table. She brought a glass of iced tea and took the chair opposite him.

"How are you?" Mrs. Wales asked in a way that meant she really wanted to know.

"Pretty good. I'm not used to it. I keep thinking I ought to write him."

She talked about the death of her father and that, a few months later, of her mother. "I was only three. I don't know what I remember and what comes from pictures and things people told me. But my parents were young and happy; in my memory they are surrounded by color. They were Armenian, met over there. He had her sent over here and married her. I'm sure it was hard for them to learn new ways. Maybe they wore themselves out learning. Probably Mama died from loneliness or fear of being so far from home." She closed her eyes, smiling. "I treasure the memory of them. Why I bet she wasn't any more than twenty-two when she died. She married at fourteen."

"Can you talk Armenian?"

"Sure, my aunts and uncles taught me." She rattled off some funny-sounding sentences, and they both laughed.

Mrs. Wales nodded toward the basket. "She says you are having an anniversary picnic."

Dave was puzzled.

"She says a six weeks anniversary."

Dave shrugged. He knew his face was red. He rocked back and forth on the chair's hind legs. "Can I ask you something just between us and you not think bad of me?"

"All right."

Dave could not look at her. "The morning they ran the

newsreel for us, Mary was standing back of the last row of seats, all by herself."

Mrs. Wales touched the ice floating in the tea and made it circle the inside of her glass.

"I kissed her, and it wasn't just a friendly kiss. I kissed her like . . . ." Dave could not decide how to put it. "It was real kissing. You know? She was crying, and she acted like she wanted to be kissed that way. I would have probably just kept on if she hadn't pulled loose." He swallowed hard.

"And you wonder if it was wrong?"

"I knew it was wrong before I did it, wrong to Sue and George, and wrong to her."

"And you don't understand why you did it." She got up and filled the sugar bowl from a red and white can. From the back she looked as Sue would in twenty years, full-bodied, the right width across the hips, with brown, round legs and arms. "Well, David, be careful of quick judgments about right and wrong. People love people in different ways. And they show different kinds of love in different ways. And sometimes, when things are out of joint, they get mixed up and pick the wrong way to show their love." She put the sugar bowl on the table and sat down.

"You think it's okay then?"

"I think Mary knows you love her in one way, because of George." She made him look at her now. "And she knows your love for Sue is a different kind."

Dave was stunned; she could not know what he felt for Sue. He laughed and did not know why. "You think I love Sue?"

"I think you do."

Dave laced his fingers behind his head and grinned at the ceiling. "Hey, is Sarge an Armenian, too?"

She snorted. "Cecil? Mercy, no." She considered for a moment. "I don't guess he's anything."

They went far out that night, beyond the lake, down into that part of Wake County where Simeon Totten got himself hanged. Dave picked someone's out-back pasture and spread the blanket, anchoring the corners with rocks against what little wind there was. Sue sat on her heels and rummaged inside the basket. Dave could see some distant Armenian ancestor kneeling over the meal she was preparing or the garment she was washing or the child she was tending. He said, "Sue, I love you."

Later, since it was a special occasion, they sat on the porch of old Steve Turner's house and ate two sandwiches. Speedy Thomas saw them and parked the squad car with the motor running and the radio on and asked did their folks know they were messing around a vacant house at two a.m. Sue told him they were glad he stopped by since it was an anniversary, and Speedy sat down and had half a pickle and a piece of chocolate cake that had been carried over from the first picnic and complained about a Folger's coffee can spitoon that he claimed Dave had left in the park.

The Author

June Rayfield Welch was born in Brownwood, Texas, in 1927. He graduated from Gainesville High School, attended Texas Christian University on football scholarship, flunked out, served in the Merchant Marine and the Army, graduated from TCU with a Bachelor of Arts degree, was a secretary to Senator Lyndon B. Johnson, was a member of the United States Capitol Police Force, graduated with the Doctor of Jurisprudence degree from George Washington University, the Master of Arts from Texas Tech University, and the Bachelor of Arts from the University of Texas at Arlington. He practiced law fifteen years, was Academic Dean of the University of Dallas for two years, and has been chairman of the Department of History and associate professor of history at the University of Dallas for the past four years. His books are **A Family History** (1965), **The Texas Courthouse** (1971), **Texas: New Perspectives** (1971), and **Historic Sites of Texas** (1972). He is an Air Force Reserve lieutenant colonel.